On the Banks of the Pampa

Praise for *On the Banks of the Pampa*

'An exquisite tapestry of light and shade, an intense evocation of nature and myth, a novel of many hues—a masterpiece.'

—NAMITA GOKHALE, author of *Paro, Shakuntala* and *Things to Leave Behind*

'In her new poetic novel, Volga combines lyrical language and the love of nature with a fearlessly critical vision of timeless issues such as caste discrimination, territorial expansion, and the thoughtless destruction of nature. As usual, she has depicted classic characters from the Ramayana—Rama, Sabari, Kabanda and Hanuma, among others—from an original and surprising angle to create a deeply thought-provoking book.'

—CHITRA BANERJEE DIVAKARUNI, author of *The Palace of Illusions, The Forest of Enchantments* and *Independence*

'This book is a deeply meaningful reimagining of the encounter between Rama and Sabari, full of questions that we need to ask ourselves today. In Volga's work, it is always women who hold wisdom and knowledge and here, her feminist perspective is as firm and confident as ever, without being strident. Purnima Tammireddy modulates this important voice beautifully so that its challenges and subversions ring loud and clear in English.'

—ARSHIA SATTAR, author of *Maryada: Searching for Dharma in the Ramayana*

On the Banks of the Pampa

A NOVEL

VOLGA

Translated from the Telugu by
PURNIMA TAMMIREDDY

HARPERPERENNIAL
An Imprint of HarperCollins *Publishers*

First published in India by Harper Perennial 2025
An imprint of HarperCollins *Publishers*
HarperCollins *Publishers* India, Cyber City,
Building 10-A, Gurugram, Haryana – 122002, India
www.harpercollins.co.in

2 4 6 8 10 9 7 5 3 1

P-ISBN: 978-93-6989-401-7
E-ISBN: 978-93-6989-292-1

Typeset in 11.5/16 Adobe Caslon Pro
by HarperCollins *Publishers* India Pvt. Ltd

Printed and bound at
Replika Press Pvt. Ltd.

FSC
www.fsc.org
MIX
Paper | Supporting
responsible forestry
FSC™ C016779

This book is produced from independently certified FSC® paper to ensure responsible forest management.

HarperCollins *Publishers*, Macken House, 39/40 Mayor Street Upper, Dublin 1, D01 C9W8, Ireland

AUTHOR'S DEDICATION

To my best friends, Dr Vemuri Krishnamurti and Dr Vemuri Shobha Rani

TRANSLATOR'S DEDICATION

To Sai Padma
—because your belief carried me through

CONTENTS

1

The darkness in the forest was so dense that not even dawn could dispel it entirely. The rays of the morning sun, further ablaze by a zealous determination, sought to usher daylight into this unlit jungle. But Surya's long-held desire to crown this region with daylight remained unfulfilled, as his prowess was a bane to his ambition.

As Surya asserted his dominance in the woods, the saplings grew stronger. They matured into large trees, their lush boughs spreading everywhere. Intoxicated by the sunlight they derived through their offshoots, the trees thickened excessively. As a result, they formed a trellis that stifled the free passage of light, allowing it to seep only through narrow, slender paths. The centuries-old trees swayed their heads and bowed to Surya to show their camaraderie and respect towards him. Impressed by these gestures, Surya veiled himself behind the clouds, displaying his benevolence.

The clouds, captivated by the forest's allure, showered down every drop of rain they possessed. The drenched trees, reinvigorated by the loving raindrops, grew with greater vigour. Exasperated from having to contain all the rain, Mother Earth released the excess water into thin streams and streamlets, guiding their way to the Pampa. The waterfalls from faraway hills also gushed into the river, teeming with life, with all kinds of species thriving in its surroundings.

This morning, the forest was abuzz with the sounds of birds chirping, peacocks screaming and elephants trumpeting. Elephants gathered beneath the banyan and peepal canopies, their skins gleaming in hues that echoed the deep, weathered barks of the trees. They rubbed their bodies against the massive tree trunks and bantered with them, revelling in their own delight. All the birds in the forest were friends with the tuskers. They flew to the spot where these majestic beasts stood, circled over their heads and shook hands with them. Deer were in a deep slumber under the ganuga trees. The does continued to feel around for their fawns even in their sleep. At a distance delicate ponna flowers blossomed and fell from the trees, turning the ground into a fragrant, sweet-smelling carpet. Rabbits and squirrels, true to their mischievous nature, trampled over this delicate tapestry. But all their naughty attempts were foiled as the flowers kept falling, creating the carpet afresh.

Cuckoos began to sing, perhaps from the mango trees ahead. Wild creatures familiar with the orchestra hurried in that direction. Both sides of their path were filled with ganneru trees in full bloom, in myriad colours—some white, some yellow, and many more in faded red.

There was hardly a tree not laden with fruits or flowers. It was a spectacular display of colour. The wealth of flowers, the wealth of fruits, and the pulsating wealth of countless life forms—there was no treasure absent there.

Mother Earth was overwhelmed and captivated witnessing her own wealth. If someone were to strike up a conversation with her and ask, 'O Mother, do you feel fulfilled when you see all your offspring in their full glory?', she would have simply burst into laughter. She would say:

'You only see the forms of consciousness that are on my surface—the singing birds, the sweet-smelling flowers, the blooming trees and the dancing animals. But have you ever wondered about the lives that exist within my belly? There are precious minerals, diamonds and gems that are yet to be discovered. Have you ever considered the possibility of life existing in every atom of my being? How amazed you would be if you could see it all!'

Today, undeterred by the forest's towering trees, Surya was leisurely wandering along the banks of the Pampa. A rocky boundary had barred the flow of the river, creating a small pond. The lotuses, native to the pond, were enchanted by the music of their honey-seeking guests, the bees. The sun's rays danced nimbly on the water, ripples the shape of tiny flowers forming on its surface. These flowers regaled the Pampa with tales from the forest. The quivering water, blithely clinging on to the weightless specks of light, begged them not to depart. 'No, we can't stay on,' said the light-streaks, adding enticingly, 'Instead, let us take you along on a journey, on the highways of the sky!'

The region was brimming with love and companionship. Nature, in its entirety, moved in harmony, and in delicate equilibrium.

As a woman walked towards the riverbank, any doubts about the presence of humans in the forest were proven false. She blended with nature seamlessly. All species capable of movement regarded her as a part of themselves. She entered the wilderness with such poise and detachment that it seemed as though she were affirming her inherent connection to this breathtakingly beautiful world. Just as one could not determine the age of the trees in this forest, they could not ascertain hers either. Despite her frail, ageing body, her gait revealed the firm control she still had over it. Her eyes exuded a glow that seemed to illumine her entire being. Her skin was dark, her hair white. The light shimmered on her dark skin, like it would on the leaves—a deep green, fading to a near-black on the trees. She resembled a tree heading to the banks of the Pampa on foot. Her name was Sabari.

The waters of the Pampa were crystal clear, reflecting anything that peered into them. They gently introduced the curious observer to the aquatic life within. These exchanges promptly turned into friendships. Every underwater creature was Sabari's confidant. She strolled along the banks of the river at a leisurely pace and filled her pot with water. She picked the lotuses that invited her with a smile. Then, bidding farewell to the river with a promise that she would return soon, she headed to the ashram—her home.

2

Sabari was not born in this forest, but she was here since childhood. How long ago did she arrive here? Neither she, nor the forest, nor Pampa—none could remember. If Maharshi Matanga had been alive, he might have revealed the answer as he was the oldest in the region. It was he who introduced Sabari to this forest. Soon, his ashram became her home. Under his guidance, she became acquainted with every tree and flower, snake and anthill, bird and worm, the home of every creature in the forest. She discovered ways to make her way to the waterfalls cascading down the hills, learned to embrace them.

Sabari had spent much of her life in Matanga Muni's ashram, learning countless forms of knowledge from him. She spent her days serving the ascetic. She tended to him in his final days, as his vision faded and his body grew frail. Following his demise, which was many years ago, there was no one left in the ashram but Sabari.

A number of forest dwellers, or aranyavasis, who held the muni in high regard, travelled long distances for a divine sight of him. Sabari ensured that their stay was comfortable. The visitors and residents of the ashram bonded over long conversations. Those from distant lands would bring news and updates from their regions. Matanga Muni would then explain the underlying, unstated meanings of these fresh developments, providing the listeners with new insights that could otherwise have eluded them. After expressing gratitude for the perspectives they gained, the visitors would bow to him and leave.

Maharshi Matanga had come to the forest at the peak of his youth, enraged and agitated. He had arrived carrying the weight of many a mortifying abasement. He was the very image of helplessness. In due course of time, he transformed himself into a brilliant beam of light that enhanced the beauty of this already exquisite forest. He often regaled Sabari, the occupants of the ashram and the aranyavasis, with the story of his transformation. Every time the ashram had a new visitor, he would narrate the story without a sign of boredom, completely immersed in the telling. Sabari listened to every iteration with unwavering devotion. Once the muni left the mortal world, the responsibility of recounting his story fell on Sabari. After all, it was her story too.

The forest's inhabitants, whether humans or beasts, greatly admired and revered Sabari. They were eager to assist her in any way they could. But she would gently refuse their help. 'I'll gladly rely on you when I'm drained of all energy. For now, let me do what I do on my own,' she would say. All who wished to lend a hand would step back and leave the ashram, not wanting to disobey her. But not Kabanda. After Matanga Muni's passing, Kabanda never explicitly stated that he would be the ashram's new caretaker, but he did everything necessary to keep things going. Sabari could not deny his assistance either because she was aware of his respect for her. Theirs was a strange bond.

Kabanda used to visit the ashram occasionally when Matanga Muni was alive. He was fond of wandering off to faraway forests. Every six months he would return to the ashram and share with Matanga Muni and Sabari all that he had seen and experienced. Three or four months would pass and he would again bid farewell to the wise elders and leave for his next expedition.

Kabanda, who could never stay in one place for long, not once left the vicinity of the ashram now. And even if he did, he would be gone only for an hour or two. Sabari had tried her best to dissuade him from this newfound habit of staying put in the ashram, but eventually, she let him be. In time, she got used to Kabanda's presence.

They reminisced about their conversations with Matanga Muni and, together, admired the splendour of the forest.

This morning, when Sabari returned to the ashram after fetching water from the river, she found Kabanda waiting there with a guest. It was common for the ashram to have visitors. Travellers passing through the forest chose the ashram as a retreat to rest awhile in. This was the first halt for travellers from the north, and they had to walk many miles more to reach another inhabited place. Sabari's abode thus welcomed unexpected guests from time to time. After enjoying the hospitality at the ashram, they would resume their journeys.

Sabari took notice of her new guest. The sweat on his body indicated that he had arrived not too long ago. He had perhaps washed his dust-covered feet at the ashram's entrance—they were still damp.

The guest was holding a tumbler of water that Kabanda must have offered him; it was still half full. Sabari placed the pot she had been carrying on the ground and adorned the surroundings with the flowers she had collected from the river. Numerous fruit-bearing trees, each laden with abundance, wreathed the ashram. Sabari plucked some fruits, offered them to the guest on a leaf plate and sat before him. The moment she did, all the birds, squirrels and rabbits gathered around her. A rabbit hopped on to her lap and proudly looked around at the other beings, as though revelling in his accomplishment. The others attempted to leap on to Sabari's lap for the coveted seat, but Kabanda sprang to ward off the creatures swiftly in an attempt to shield Sabari.

All the animals stopped in their tracks, almost as if they had realized their mistake. Kabanda took the rabbit from Sabari's hand and said, 'Don't you know you must put on your best behaviour when guests are here? Now, go and play elsewhere.'

The wildlings ambled away.

The guest watched these interactions in wonder. Sabari said to him, 'You must be hungry. You look fatigued. Please have these fruits.'

The man ate all that had been offered to him and thanked Sabari, joining his palms in a namaskaram, his face radiant.

Sabari leaned closer to him and asked, 'Where are you coming from?'

The guest's features and complexion had piqued her curiosity, for they did not match those of the people from the south. Clearly, he was not from the region, and she knew that only people from far-off places brought exciting news.

'I come from the north, Amma. My name is Sutapa. I hail from the city of Ayodhya.' Sabari's face grew troubled, but only for a brief moment.

'I'm surprised to hear you've been travelling alone all the way from the city to the remote shores of the Pampa, deep within the forest. These days, aranyavasis seem to be more inclined to travel to the ever-expanding cities, sprouting across our region too. What made you turn away from all that and lose yourself in these woods?'

Sutapa sighed deeply and said, 'Now, that's a long story. Our king was Maharaja Dasharatha. We hoped he'd follow tradition and abdicate the throne in his old age, passing it on to his eldest son, Ramachandra. Who knows what transpired in the queens' chambers, but the king ordered that Ramachandra be exiled to the forests and, his third queen's son, Bharata, be crowned as the king instead. Without putting up a fight for his rights, Ramachandra left for the forest with his wife Sita and brother Lakshmana.

'When word of our beloved prince's exile reached us, the Ayodhyavasis, we lost all hope and were no longer interested to continue living in the city. We, too, wanted to follow Ramachandra into the forests. Many of us started our expeditions under these circumstances. But once he realized our intent, Ramachandra forbade us to follow him. While several complied with his wishes and returned to the city, some of us broke away from the group and took another path into the forest. Many months and many miles later, some decided to return home.

Those of us who wanted to continue scattered in different directions.

'A few travellers stopped at places that caught their attention. I'm driven by the desire to visit the sea, and my journey will end only when I reach there. I pause occasionally when fatigue gets the better of me. This forest, nestled along the banks of the Pampa, is so serene that I couldn't walk past it. I've never encountered anything like it. My hope is to halt here for four days before continuing on my way. I'm blessed to find myself at the same ashram where Matanga Muni once lived.'

Sabari heard everything he said with astonishment. Kabanda was stunned as well. 'How incredible!' he said, stepping outside soon after to attend to something that needed his attention.

Sabari reflected on Sutapa's story. He had ventured into the woods following his wronged prince, driven solely by sorrow. In time, he became a wanderer because he fell in love with the forests. Prince Ramachandra was not his priority any more. From starting the journey out of loyalty to his prince, Sutapa's ambition evolved into crossing the rivers and forests to reach the sea. His journey was no longer materialistic but spiritual, Sabari thought. Her interest grew in Ramachandra, who had forsaken his rajyam—his kingdom—to live in the forest.

Rajyam!—she mused—it's a desire you can't reverse! A thirst you can't quench! Abandoning it is not a feat you expect of ordinary beings. Ramachandra, whoever he might be, must be exceptional, she thought.

After showing Sutapa a suitable place to rest, Sabari sat under a kadimi tree to unwind.

The jungle was almost silent. The soft hum of birds chirping in the distance was pleasing to the ears. Overcome by weariness, Sabari rested some. She had been losing energy of late. Ageing inevitably brings with it a certain set of challenges. Nobody can defeat it. Sabari was not hoping for such a conquest in any case, though. She had been waiting for the day she would become one with the boundless nature. However, the changes she had been witnessing around her were causing her intense distress. She wished there was a remedy to her agony.

In the forests of the Pampa, humans had always lived in harmony with other creatures. They ate what was available and were content with that. The fruits and vegetables were seasonal. The locals were fond of the fish from the waterfalls and streams of the Pampa. They feasted on a variety of fish and prawns. But no matter how much they consumed, the river continued to swell with marine life. Rabbits, wild cocks and, sometimes, deer were hunted down and made into delicious fare. On special occasions, they had the meat of cranes and other birds.

The sweet waters of the Pampa and the fresh air of the forest ensured the well-being of the people. Everything was in plenty, nothing was lacking. Some offered prayers to nature in an attempt to uncover its secrets, some would be busy practising singing and dancing, and still others were occupied making vessels and assorted tools for daily use.

Everybody loved playing games. Swimming across the streams, trekking the hills, running along the fields and climbing up the trees in competition with animals were some of the many sports they enjoyed. There were disputes, but on rare occasions. The aranyavasis strove to resolve the conflicts among themselves.

There was no discrimination between men and women; chores were not marked by gender. The people in the forest were free to mate with whomever they preferred. If babies were born out of such unions, there would be widespread celebrations. Introducing children to the forest early and helping them bond with nature was an integral part of their lives.

Everything on the banks of the Pampa was peaceful and serene until the menace called rajyam invaded their lives. In nearby jungles, the formidable built their centres of dominion. They began building cities. They stripped the forest for miles on end—cutting down the old, strong trees. Levelled the land, blasted through rock, carved out stones and hauled them to the cities. They gouged the riverbeds, ripping away layer after layer of sand…

Sabari, who was resting under the kadimi tree, recollected all that was transpiring with a heavy heart. She was well aware of the perils of power and the acts of cruelty carried out in the name of rajyam from her early childhood. In an effort to push aside the memories and the misery they brought, Sabari gazed upwards. A bright smile broke across her face. Above her was a sky of leaves, with light seeping through the green, blinking like stars which had let slip from memory that it was broad daylight. Sabari lay flat on her back. It was a sight to behold.

In her tranquil state of mind, she continued to repose and lost track of time until she remembered Sutapa. Their guest must have been waiting for her after his siesta.

Sabari reached her cottage using a walking stick, which helped her quicken her pace. By the time she reached the ashram, Sutapa and Kabanda were already engaged in conversation.

Upon seeing Sabari, Kabanda said, 'Amma! I'm getting to know more about Ramachandra. It's not common for someone to give up their kingdom, right? After all, aren't we witnessing an unyielding desire for rajyam? Aren't we familiar with its atrocities? Ramachandra is from a place where people are cultured and civilized. But these nagariks seem to have lost the innate human capacity for genuinely loving and caring for one another. It's a place where, over the centuries, the natural impulse to help and uplift others has withered so completely that kindness now persists only through rulebooks, and harm is avoided not out of conscience, but through formal prohibitions. There are mechanisms in place to keep an eye on individuals, enabling both violence and peace—depending on what suits them. The place is so rife with signs of civilization, what they call nagarikata, that warfare has become a standard way of expanding territories. Ramachandra's willingness to give up his throne and his choice to go into exile to the forests instil hope in me, Amma!' A childlike enthusiasm brought a sparkle to Kabanda's eyes.

Sabari agreed with Kabanda and asked Sutapa, 'You didn't tell us why your prince chose to leave his kingdom.'

'Even before we had any knowledge of what had transpired in the inner chambers of the palace, Ramachandra was walking the streets in austere clothing, unbecoming of a prince. We followed him weeping…' Sutapa recollected the scene despondently, as if hoping he had only dreamt it.

'Were you so fond of him that you followed him into the forest?' Sabari asked in surprise.

'I don't know, Amma! Back then, I had no idea that I'd travel this far. Our main concern till we crossed the Sarayu river was Ramachandra. But once we were in the depths of the forests, I couldn't remember anything that passed before. It felt like the woods were calling out to me. The thought of settling down somewhere for good or returning home didn't occur to me. A fellow traveller suggested, "If you go further south, you will come upon wonderful groves spreading endlessly. Once you can cross them all, there will be a vast, infinite sea." I'm on a journey towards the sea; I yearn for the sight of boundless waters.'

Sabari smiled softly. 'I bless you with all my heart that your wish comes true.' Then, she gently reminded Kabanda about some tasks that needed carrying out to make their guest feel welcome.

'Kabanda was hinting at the story of Matanga Muni's first visit here a long time ago…' Sutapa said hesitantly. Sabari looked down in silence.

'It seems you came to these banks along with the muni,' he added.

For some inexplicable reason, Sabari felt like sharing everything about Matanga Muni with Sutapa. Anyone could benefit from his story, but Sutapa seemed to be a man full of wanderlust. If he spread the story of her guru during his travels across regions, his teachings would reach more people. Matanga Muni's story could not slip into oblivion—they could not let it. Not while Kabanda and she were still around.

'I'll tell you everything, Sutapa! Some parts of the story, I've only heard from other people. To the other parts, I've been a witness. A few aspects of the story, I fathomed myself. I hope you consider sharing this story with many more people. Matanga Muni ought to be a chiranjeeva—immortal! Besides, what can bring me more pleasure than sharing stories of the past at my ripe and ready-to-drop-dead age? But first, you must rest. There's plenty of time for our chats,' Sabari said and ambled away towards the banks of the Pampa.

3

A wave of relief washed over Sabari as she settled on the banks of the Pampa. Memories of the past flooded her heart and mind at Sutapa's curious enquiry about Matanga Muni. Her life had been completely different until she reached the shores of this river. Matanga Muni's journey, too, had been one of its kind. Yet, the Pampa and its forests offered them much needed comfort and solace.

Sabari remembered her childhood quite well. Were those days so easy to forget? Sabari's father, Kannudu, and mother, Kabari, were aranyavasis, the jungle's offspring. She was a doting sister to two elder brothers. Until the age of ten, her life was free of worry. The year she turned ten was the year her childhood was snatched from her. Sabari was a witness to everything that unfolded. She saw her world crumble before her with her own eyes.

An army, wielding weapons, invaded the forest in which Sabari's family lived. The attackers began killing the inhabitants as soon as they spotted them. Sabari ended up being a spectator of one such atrocious incident, but her parents were swift enough to take her away from the scene and escape for the time being. Nobody knew who the attackers were or what they wanted from the aranyavasis, and that increased the confusion, chaos and concern in their minds. Never had they known such a terrifying invasion and commotion in their lives. The perpetrators settled in tents at a distance to rest. Everything was peaceful for a few hours.

Some of the youngsters from the forest discreetly jumped from one treetop to another and watched what occupied the men in the shelters. The offenders were busy feasting and drinking. Some practised sword fighting.

The young spies returned to inform the elders what they had seen. Everyone was consumed by one question: What do we do next? It was evident that the invaders were from the city. Sabari's grandfather was very well aware of city-dwellers, nagaravasis as they were called. She sat in his lap and listened to everything he had to say about them with rapt attention.

Sabari's grandfather, that is, Kannudu's father, was Munnudu. When he was young, Munnudu had set off on a journey to explore the outskirts of the forest, but never returned. At eighteen, he was imprisoned by nagaravasis and taken along to the city. He ended up as a slave there—a slave shorn of any human dignity. The tasks he was asked to carry out were beyond his, or anyone else's, imagination. Munnudu was fully convinced that every single job forced upon him was sinful. He refused to act on their commands. His masters tortured him endlessly to get him to do their bidding. They made him dig into the earth till pataal lok—the netherworld—was visible. They made him cut down the strongest of trees. Unwilling to execute their abominable orders, Munnudu attempted to cut off his own hands instead. As punishment for his act of dissent, Munnudu was directed to behead those who had become slaves before him and had lost their hands or legs in battles or during mining activities. They were of no use to the nagaravasis any longer; they had become a burden. Munnudu and other young slaves were thus handed the sharpest of swords and knives to finish them off.

A few years later, Munnudu's masters noticed that his vitality was fading, so they assigned him domestic work in one of their houses instead of tasks involving intense manual labour, like mining. He was repulsed by the master's indolence, the unsavoury ways in which he indulged in luxury, and yet, he tolerated it all. He had no choice.

It was only a matter of two years before another city attacked the city Munnudu had been serving in. He was forced to wield a sword in battle at his master's behest. But he found a way to escape in the midst of all the fighting. Munnudu ran without knowing where he was headed, but was determined not to stop running until he found himself amidst thick wilderness. It was only after a while that he realized he was running towards yet another city instead of a forest. There was no sign of vegetation or water anywhere in sight. There was no question of finding a fruit, root vegetable, a rabbit, or any other creature, nothing that he could douse his hunger with. The whole area looked tonsured. The path was so narrow that only a single horse could gallop on it. The more he ran, the more his destination evaded him. The road coiled around him like a relentless python.

Munnudu never cared about the sun, never succumbed to the cold; he enjoyed getting drenched in the rain. He could control his hunger and thirst. As the forest he was searching for continued to elude him, the unnerving barren area, in all its nakedness, filled him with fear. If he ran into any nagariks again, all his hopes of returning home would be gone.

Days passed—three, four or five? Munnudu had stopped counting. On the seventh day, he could finally spot some vegetation. He was elated to see leafy shades of trees and pools of water. Roaring with happiness, he jumped into a pool. After drinking as much as his belly could take, he bathed in the water till the heat of his body and mind calmed significantly. He jumped into another pool again, agile like a deer. Afterwards, breathing in the forest air, devoid of the foul smells of the city, he slept like a log.

Munnudu had shared this story with his clan many times. As he described in vivid detail the smoke of the city and the stifling darkness of the pataal lok he was enslaved in, the listeners trembled in fear, they had goosebumps all over.

After escaping from the city, Munnudu found a suitable female companion in the same forest. Kannudu was born. Kannudu grew up to be a strong young man and, he, too, found a capable female companion. It seemed like Kannudu and Kabari were born for each other. They could hardly be separated from one another. Like Kannudu, Kabari was also a highly skilled hunter. She could swiftly trek up the hills without breaking a sweat. Giant trees served as their primary mode of transportation. They hopped from one tree to another. It was only after Sabari's birth that they decided to have a roof over their heads. The couple started rearing cows and goats, and planting seeds in a small field. They grew vegetables and fruits, and enjoyed an abundance of honey and milk.

Some days, the food was in excess. But there were also days when nothing was available. The aranyavasis could, however, conserve their energy efficiently even if they ate only once in two or four days. After relishing what was at hand, they prayed to Mother Forest—an energy they believed was a goddess—to bless them with plentiful food.

In the days when water was scarce, they would treasure every drop of water. They, along with the other creatures of the forest, waited with quiet anticipation for the rain. Until they could see the first set of clouds in the sky, they sought refuge in silence. Hardly any sound emerged from the settlements except the occasional crying and laughing, and the playful shrieks of the children. The forest reciprocated their way of living. From the trees to the plants, the ants to the elephants, every being was still and silent—as if praying and meditating with the earth and sky as their focus. The sound of their footsteps was almost imperceptible.

A few days slipped by, and swarms of clouds gathered in the skies, their movements stirring the air with a symphony of rhythmic sounds. Everyone—not just human beings, but every single being—jumped and screamed with joy. They let their parched bodies soak up every bit of the rain and began to dance. Several festivities celebrating water—

the rain, the streams, the waterfalls and the rivers—commenced; the forest rejoiced.

There were fewer tragedies in the lives of those living in the forest. Death was the call of the earth, the air, the fire, the water and the sky. It meant migrating to the skies. The aranyavasis believed that the dead were blessed with the power of invisibility, and could watch and protect them from the skies. When overcome with sadness, they cried their hearts out. Events of birth and death were not occasions exuding differing emotions. They accepted both, with gratitude and great respect, as nature's gifts.

Nagaravasis did not appreciate such ways of life. To them, the choices of those inhabiting the forests were uncivilized, primitive—far from nagarikata, hence anagarik. They had to justify the 'civilized' way of life, and thus felt the need to ridicule the aranyavasis. That is why they invaded the forests, islands and hills. They did not revere the earth as a mother goddess but saw it as a mine brimming with buried treasures. They were never content, no matter how many crops it bore. In their eyes, the earth should yield and yield, copiously and ceaselessly. They inflicted pain and terror on the earth, compelling it to produce beyond its capacity. They were not satisfied till the land became barren, having reaped too much in too little time.

The earth ended up as an object of research for the nagaravasis—it became a plaything. It turned into a fount of temptation that stirred a desire for conquest. Their growing curiosity and thirst for greater knowledge drove them to explore what more could be uncovered and extracted from the earth. Their gods existed solely to grant them endless boons.

Nagaravasis considered trees, flowers, the sky, the sun, the moon, summer, moonlight, rain, and everything else as existing solely for their amusement. Praying to nature was considered foolish if these natural elements did not act according to their needs and fancies. To them, the true meaning of civilization was to rule nature. They felt compelled to find man-made ways to make it rain when there was none. They diverted a river's natural course, holding its waters captive for the future, built marble buildings to save themselves from exposure to sunlight, and so on.

So worked the minds of the torchbearers of nagarikata. There existed among the nagariks some who would not tread their path, but such anagariks were few and far between. This unsophisticated lot lived to be discriminated against. They were allowed to be around only to serve, to get chased away, even to be killed.

Slaying, torturing, and discovering more and more forms of brutality were the goals of nagarikata, its ultimate purpose. Without violence, murder, rape, war and exploitation, there was no civilization.

Munnudu informed Kannudu about the evil ways in which nagarikata thrived. Kannudu was anxious about the nagaravasis' invasion of their area. He shared his concerns with a few others in his tribe and proposed moving deeper into the woods for a few days.

'Let's see,' was the only response he got from the others.

The aranyavasis lived unhurried lives. They watched the sun rise without a single worry nagging them. They could patiently watch a flower bloom at its own sweet pace. They were capable of spending a whole day either sleeping peacefully or working tirelessly. That was why they did not hasten to move deeper into the woods.

However, the nagariks were restless. Being still was beyond them. Desires and fancies chased them like the waves of a sea. They could not relish food, they could not sleep soundly. Their only ambition was to satisfy hunger and sleep, going through the motions mechanically. But the dreams they ran after distracted them so much that even these basic needs remained unsatiated. They thought time raced forward, never letting them pause. The truth, however, was that it was they who refused to let time pause.

They were the ones who believed it must never be allowed to stop. They could not imagine the possibility that time could actually stand still.

Without wasting any time, the nagariks took another route to approach the aranyavasis: they invited the local tribal leaders—of the inhabitants under siege—seeking a dialogue with them.

A group, comprising four elderly tribal leaders and four young men, made their way to the tents where the nagaravasis were camped. Despite their fears, they were greeted with warmth. They were placed in high seats, offered unusual and eccentric food and drinks, and presented with precious silks and expensive jewels. The heightened emotions of the aranyavasis began to soften because of these amicable gestures.

'Sirs, who are you, and where are you from? Why have you not sought to talk to us before killing our men?' the tribals asked with all the gentleness they were capable of. Though their anger knew no bounds remembering how their people had been slain, they warned each other with their eyes that they would keep calm.

They were appalled at what the war chief of the nagaravasis had to say. After discussing the leader's proposal among themselves, one of the tribal leaders gave the remaining seven members a concise summary of what they had grasped of the leader's words. It was not easy to wrap one's head around the words of the civilized. However, the representatives of the tribe were not inclined to give up easily and did their best to gauge the real intention behind those convoluted words. The young men were inexperienced. While patience was the forte of the seniors, the younger lot were restless and easily agitated.

It took close to an hour to draw any firm conclusions. Finally, one of the leaders explained to the others:

The invaders were from a city on the other side of the forest, where they had been living for many years. However, their population had grown exponentially. Their streets got crowded. There was not nearly enough water for irrigation, and that impacted the agricultural produce, resulting in a shortage of foodgrains. The only solutions they could conceive for all these problems were to occupy the forest, expand the city, convert parts of the forest into arable land and divert water from the rivers to the streams for irrigation.

As if their motives were not offensive enough, the invaders talked disparagingly about aranyavasis during the negotiation, raising their tempers. Now that their intentions were crystal clear, the representatives felt an acute tension. The tribal leader who had been explaining the situation to the others in his group so far now repeated the rival leader's words to rid his companions of any confusion they might still have had regarding the nagaravasis' proposal.

'All of you are anagarik. There's no meaning to your lives. You don't have houses, backyards or highways. You don't know how to till land and harvest crops. You aren't animals, but your lives are hardly different from theirs. If you accept our offer of friendship, we'll give you land and teach you cultivation. We'll build your houses for you. Go ahead and cut all the trees in this forest. Flatten the land. We'll ensure you get your fair share of it. But the decision of how much each one of you will get lies with us. We'll provide you with food while you work for us. You lot aimlessly roam the woods because you have no work. You aren't disciplined. You eat whatever you see hanging from a tree. You starve on days when you can't find any food. We'll teach you how to preserve and store for your rainy days. We'll show you what nagarikata in its finest form looks like.

'To be honest, the food shortage we're facing isn't as acute, but it will become worse in the next decade or so. We had anticipated the possibility of such a reality. We aim to extend our city into this forest and convert it into arable land. You don't know how to preserve anything. You don't know what wealth is. Nagarikata is nothing but the art of mastering these. If you cooperate with us, we'll give you special status as our subjects and govern you. Imagine what a great honour and privilege it'd be for folks like you. Should you opt not to support us, it's no matter.

We wouldn't hesitate to wipe you off the face of the forest for good. Don't doubt our claims of possessing countless weapons, nor our clan's exceptional talent in crafting new ones. We're trained in numerous combat techniques. Weapons are the sole means to defend a civilization. Yours are laughable—scarcely fit to even hunt down a tiger!'

The tribals found it hard to remain calm and level-headed in the face of these provocative words. Yet, they managed to respond as gently as possible.

'Why would we hunt tigers? If we don't hunt, why would we need better weapons? We do possess the skills and tools to defend ourselves. We know how to live without needing yours. We have access to abundant food—Mother Forest bestows upon us all that we need to survive. We're content with our lives. Why would we want to destroy our forest, our home? Stop trying to convince us with your foolish words and return to where you came from.'

The tribal representatives went back to their homes and had another round of discussions with a larger gathering about the exchange they had had with the nagaravasis. All present were appalled and furious, except Kannudu, who was terrified. He could not disregard the experiences of his father. The old man was well aware of not only the cities but also of the state, or rajyam. Was his life as a slave in the city forgettable by any means?

The rajyam was what backed these cities. The invaders were not merely nagaravasis, they were the rajyam. Without it, the cities would collapse.

The rajyam ran everything. And for the rajyam, borders were of paramount importance. The rajyam exerted control over any living being within its defined boundaries, with the sole purpose of domination. It strove to confine every creature within its grasp, worked relentlessly to exercise such power. The rajyam decided who got to breathe and for how long. Within its borders, it held an unrestrained sway, its authority danced to the beats of destruction. Expanding territories was its favourite game, its primary indulgence. It could neither understand nor stand a land without borders, a land without control. It drew lines. It built walls. It restricted movement.

To expand its dominion, it indulged in war—its favourite sport. The only possible outcome of this sport was either the creation of new frontiers or a change of hands in ruling power. Regardless of the hands that wielded the power, the rules remained unchanged. All decrees ensured that everybody within the territory was in the rajyam's grip—an iron grip that never loosened.

Munnudu understood that the invaders wished to bring them into the rajyam's fold, and immediately advised Kannudu to go to a safer place with Sabari and his wife. Both of Kannudu's sons were already on their own—and were more than capable of taking care of themselves and their families. Munnudu offered the same advice to the others, but only a few agreed. Most were reluctant to leave the land they had grown up in. They believed that if they all remained united, nobody could harm them. Furthermore, the idea of fleeing did not appeal to them. They preferred death over the act of running away—an act of cowardice. Munnudu, too, did not have it in him to run away. Besides, no one could understand and decipher the rajyam's moves and the nagaravasis' strategies as well as he could. He informed Kannudu that he and his wife would stay back and urged him to escape with Sabari as soon as possible.

In four days, Kannudu discovered another thick forest within walking distance. He passed the information to the rest of the tribe and asked them to flee to this place if they sensed even the slightest danger. He requested the tribe to look after his parents with a promise that he would visit them from time to time. With Sabari sitting atop his shoulders and while minding the four cows he was rearing, Kannudu left home with his wife. Two wild dogs followed them.

4

Kannudu encountered Matanga while he was making a small tent for his family in the thick forest. Matanga was fasting for his penance. Kannudu was familiar with such ascetics in the forest from which he had escaped. Except for greeting them with folded hands, the aranyavasis knew no other way to interact with sages. One day, Kannudu had just managed to finish building a roof over their heads when Matanga fainted. Kannudu brought him to his house and restored him to health by serving him water, milk and medicinal herbs.

As Kannudu continued to serve him, Matanga regained his health and was soon back on his feet. When he began his practice of penance again, Sabari was already playing in his lap, addressing him as 'Tatha!', as she would her grandfather. Kannudu was preparing to visit his old home when some travellers from there arrived with news that his parents were hale and hearty. Relieved, he dropped the idea of paying them a visit.

Visitors from the nearby forests showed great respect to Matanga, who was engaged in penance all day but made time in the evenings to share with them a few things he knew. He would lull Sabari to sleep by singing songs to her.

Kannudu became curious about Matanga Muni's penance: what it was for and what he hoped to attain through it. Not one to hide his curiosity, he asked him multiple times. The muni answered Kannudu's questions, his mind flooding with memories of arriving in this forest for the first time.

Matanga Muni had come to the forest in his prime, seething with humiliation. He was determined to erase the dishonour for good. His ferocity was so intense it seemed capable of setting the woods ablaze. Kannudu and others listened to his story with keen attention as he explained the reasons for his outrage. Sabari was also present there, but she was too young to understand the essence of his words then. Matanga would narrate the incidents to Sabari again when she was old enough to grasp their meaning.

'One fine day, a few years ago, I attained new wisdom. I used to live in a small settlement on the outskirts of a city. A muni in the nearby woods taught the youth of the area various skills, imparted to them knowledge. I approached him, seeking his tutelage. With a smile on his face, he bestowed upon me facts about myself. I was introduced to what the world referred to as "jnanam".

But my newly gained wisdom only brought my way mortification and misery. It disregarded my birth, considered it inconsequential. It seemed like my body and soul were consumed by fire, charred by its flames. I loathed my life, my birth, my body, my parents, my relatives and my friends. I despised myself. The blood pumping through my veins disgusted me.

'The maharshi pacified me by telling me I had a chance at redemption, that I could transform myself. My rage subsided as the wise man who deemed me an untouchable also presented suggestions to make myself worthy of respect again. I could become pious regardless of what I was born as. I could be held in high regard as a human being, a touchable! I was determined to eradicate my previous self and be reborn.

'My devotion towards my guru was such that if he had asked me to jump into a fire pit, I would have without a second thought. However, he clarified that I couldn't purify myself by going up in smoke. Instead, the enlightened one offered to show me another way, but with a condition: I must not harbour even a grain of doubt about his teachings or his intentions. Only that which is free of doubt, untouched by it, unyielding to it—that alone is irrefutable jnanam. And only such jnanam could free me from my birth, and from the blood I carry—my parents' blood.

'Following his teachings, I began my journey into the forest to attain that jnanam through penance. It seemed the only way out for me. Going to the woods and doing penance didn't cause me any distress. How could it? I was the one who had already abandoned all my worldly relations. I've been immersed in penance, faithfully abiding by the strict rules laid down by my guru. I'm hoping wisdom smiles upon me soon.'

Kannudu was astonished to hear Matanga's story. He remembered his father telling him that nagaravasis practised untouchability, through which they alienated certain people, but he was not able to grasp it fully. He was unsure about what Matanga called jnanam, but he could not see it in a positive light, as it meant despising one's roots. What wisdom could one attain by rejecting one's own birth? What could Matanga achieve by doing such a thing? The others who had assembled there to listen to the muni's story also fell silent like Kannudu. He could not comprehend the motive behind Matanga Muni's penance. Knowledge seemed precarious to him, as did cities and civilization.

Two summers had passed. The forest that Kannudu migrated from was being destroyed bit by bit. The aranyavasis, who were previously as free as the birds and animals to wander in the forest, had now become slaves. Inescapable traps were set across the woods to capture them. Munnudu had reached an advanced age. He had lost his wife, and not having his son with him during the tragedy saddened him further.

When Kannudu learned of his mother's demise, he could no longer delay his visit. Taking Kabari and Sabari with him, he began his journey to see his father. Now, the distance between the forests could be traversed in three days instead of four. But no one could say for sure how long it would take to evade the barbed wires and security personnel to enter the region.

Determined to bring his father back to his new home, Kannudu tried desperately for seven days to gain entry to the area, but failed. Kabari dismissed his suggestion that she, along with Sabari, should return home while he undertook the treacherous journey all by his lonesome.

New days did not open up any new paths. With every passing day, Kannudu grew furious. He was being restricted from stepping into the forest where he had played as a child, romanced Kabari as an adolescent and witnessed Sabari's birth as an adult. He no longer resided there, nor did he wish to return to it forever. He only hoped to take his father back with him. He had no intention of causing anyone any harm; yet he could not find a way to enter the region. Any thought of audacious behaviour to challenge the security guards would vanish the moment a playful Sabari would latch on to his legs. He could not muster the courage to desert his little one. Kabari kept insisting that the three of them would stick together no matter what.

One night, amid the pitch blackness, they finally managed to cross the barbed-wire fences. Bodies bleeding, they ran in one direction and the other, unable to work out the way to Munnudu's home in the unrecognizable landscape. As the delicate light of dawn hit them, they found themselves under a huge tree. Without wasting another second, they climbed up to hide in its lofty branches and took shelter in what was a garden of darkness. Nobody could see them. A moment of relief! They slept the rest of the morning, clinging to the branches like monkeys. The other non-human residents of the tree observed the family sleeping from a distance and chose to leave them in peace. Two big monkeys left some fruits near the new guests.

By the time Kabari awoke, the moon was in sight. A thin beam of light fell on the branch on which they were resting. Kabari could smell ripe fruits near her. In the soft glow of the faint light, she scanned the branches looking for the fruits. As soon as she found them, she secured them in the folds of her clothes. Upon waking up, Kannudu and Sabari devoured the fruits. They sat motionless, like dolls, careful not to draw any attention to themselves. Monkeys and a variety of birds came to greet them and sniffed them gently. A few snakes hissed at them amicably. The monkeys offered them palm fruits full of sweet water to quench their thirst. As dawn broke, they fell back into a deep slumber.

After sleeping for three days, during which time the tree's residents hosted them graciously, Kannudu and his family decided to resume their journey on the fourth day. Climbing down the tree was no ordeal, but where would they go next? The view from the branches was not encouraging. As far as they could see, there was only barren land with no vegetation. At a distance, a few scattered houses appeared as tiny as the stars in the sky. Who lived there? What harm could they cause to their family? The answers would reveal themselves only if they managed to reach there.

To return home by crossing the barbed wires yet again made no sense to them. Instead, the couple decided to move forward. As they took long and quick steps away from the giant tree, all the creatures there remained silent: the birds did not sing for some time, the monkeys did not move an inch, the snakes did not hiss, the insects did not stir. The gigantic tree was stock-still, as if there was some great looming danger. Not a leaf fluttered.

As they continued to walk, their bodies trembled at the sight in front of them. A vast expanse of empty land, devoid of any tree cover, as though never graced by the presence of a single green sapling! Kannudu and Kabari were familiar with the sunlight that was as gentle and kind as the moonlight, but now they felt chased by the harsh sun beating down on their backs. They, who had once considered sprinting as natural as walking, were now breathless and struggled to continue their journey. The thunderous pounding of their hearts was too unsettling to ignore.

Finally, they saw some structures at a distance. What was in store for them once they reached there? Would they get to see Kannudu's father? Would they get to see any of their kin? They were too exhausted to think, and the answers were as hazy as their vision.

Sabari hugged her father tightly. Suddenly, they flopped to the ground and lay there for a while. Only once they had gathered some strength did they rise and resume their journey, determined to face anything that would come their way. As they continued to move forward, the structures became clearer. Kannudu and Sabari were dumbfounded by what lay before them; they could not believe it was the same place in which they had once lived. Little Sabari was more than lost.

Where had the massive trees disappeared? The couple realized what cutting off trees could lead to. All the creatures living on those trees had vanished, and in their place now were rows and rows of cavelike houses belonging to the nagariks. People were moving in and out of their homes.

Four men, who were the first to come across Kannudu's family, greeted them with suspicion, eyeing them warily.

'Who are you?', 'Where have you come from?', 'What's the purpose of your visit?', 'How did you even manage to cross the borders?'…

Kannudu could not comprehend their language but could sense that the locals were enquiring about him and his family. He answered them in gestures and broken words. Upon hearing him, one of the men quickly exited the scene, while the remaining three surrounded them, mocking and taunting them.

Sabari held on to her mother's waist tightly and buried her face in her stomach. The little girl found the appearance and language of the strangers unbearable. Meanwhile, the fellow who had left in a hurry returned with another man. Kannudu and Kabari were relieved to see that the new man was a child of the forest like them. He was working as an interpreter, translating between the languages of the nagariks and the aranyavasis. He was employed to teach aranyavasis the language of the city. Not suspecting any harm from their tribesman, the couple shared everything about them with him. Soon, Kannudu's words became clearer even without interpretation, and the enraged locals shoved the family so hard that all three fell to the ground. They then commanded the family to follow them.

The interpreter, also following the family, introduced himself as Senudu and briefed Kannudu about what would happen next. According to Senudu, the four men who had been violent with them were not yet subjects of the rajyam. Anyone under its direct rule lived there with every comfort possible. The nagariks tended to see migrants as their enemies. They would first force the migrants to work for them as slaves, and only after they had gained enough trust would the migrants be elevated to the status of being subjects of the rajyam. Even after being accepted as one among them, the migrants were marked distinctly, with a green metal badge hanging around their necks, while the subjects sported yellow ones. The colour green in the badges indicated they were half-subjects, with fewer privileges and more restrictions. They could not wander around freely. They were to stay put at a designated place and dutifully perform the jobs assigned to them. Men and women were not permitted to live together and could see each other only when the officials approved. Children till the age of ten were required to live elsewhere, and the concerned authorities would provide them with food.

Hearing this, Kabari and Kannudu froze in silence. The very next moment, Kannudu took Sabari in his arms and started running in the opposite direction. Kabari, too, mustered all her strength to run behind them. For quite some time, the four men walking ahead did not realize that the family was trying to flee. Senudu, who was the first to notice them escaping, waited until the couple were at a considerably safe distance before alerting the men, careful not to endanger them by raising the alarm too soon. They created a commotion; hooting, clapping and shouting. In no time, other men on horses started to run after Kannudu from every direction. The family of three, which was already starving, distressed and exhausted, was captured within minutes of the chase.

Sabari was separated from her parents and put in a camp for children. Even the young ones here looked aged. Children, oblivious to the essence of their childhood! They had been robbed of their innocence. Some may have lived there in isolation since the age of two, so they never learned to talk. Most of them were speech impaired. The only task they were trained in was to sort and pick things from piles of soil. They were not even offered a bunch of leaves to cover themselves.

Sabari had thought of escaping from the camp from the very moment she arrived there. She was equally hopeful of her parents' breakout. The little girl hung on to these dreams so tightly that she could hardly muster the strength for anything else. She carefully observed her surroundings. The young Sabari did not exactly understand what an escape or a breakout meant, and she was clueless about how the idea had entered her mind. All she knew was she had to get out of there. And that strong desire to return home was the only thing that helped her to continue breathing.

Days flew by. The children continued to sift the soil for shining particles. In exchange, they were fed gruel daily. They were permitted to briefly sleep at night so that they could regain enough strength to work the next day. Gradually, Sabari got accustomed to the regime.

The land surrounding the camp was desolate, devoid of any trace of green. The slightest movement from the campers was enough to alert the security guards. Nobody moved an inch even in their sleep. In the darkest of nights too, there were faint rays of light, as the guards did not rest and were ever watchful.

Once, many children died in the camp. Sabari had no idea what the guards did with their bodies. They would never touch the children otherwise—they were slaves, after all, and also dirty and unkempt. After staying in the camp for over a period of two full moons, Sabari hoped she might find an escape route if she knew how they disposed of the dead bodies.

More time went by. Sabari resolved that tracking the sunrises and moonrises would be crucial for her. Earlier, the movements of the sun and the moon were an integral part of her life, but now they were so distant that she had to make an effort to remember their existence. From the moment she was born, she had bathed in rivers, plunged into lakes or stood under waterfalls seeking solace from the heat of her body. Now, she was made to wait to get two fistfuls of water to quench her thirst. Sabari's heart toughened the day she realized that, not just water, even her tears were precious.

With every passing day, the moon waned, but when it was back to the waxing phase with unmissable punctuality, it made Sabari hopeful.

Her days were filled with strenuous work, ending with long, protracted bouts of flogging. There was incomprehensible hollering in harsh voices. And then there were the innocent yet weird looks from her fellow inmates. Sabari feared that if these hardships were to continue any longer, her identity, the memories of her parents, any vestiges of her past life would get erased. As a means to remain sane and safeguard her past, her heart created a world within her. Sabari battled hard with reality to remain in this safe cocoon. Stretching her brain's muscles and veins, she tried hard to navigate through her memories, but the exercise wore her out to such an extent that she had no strength left even to take a few steps. Worried she would not be able to get up if she collapsed, she slapped and hurt herself to stay awake and keep her mind focused on revisiting and reliving the good times of the past.

During such a difficult time, a mother of a newborn arrived at the camp. It seemed to Sabari that, just like her, the woman too was trying to live in the memories of her past. She went and sat by her side. The mother was not even keen on breastfeeding her infant. Sabari gestured to her, silently asking whether she wanted to escape from the camp. For a while, the mother was unable to understand Sabari's signals. When she finally could, there was a spark in her eyes that could have lighted up the entire camp for days on end, if only it could have been retained. But alas, the glint disappeared in no time. However, the jolt that fleeting light had sent through the woman's body and the surge of inspiration it had given her were immense. She would not leave Sabari even for a moment, following her like a shadow. She sat where Sabari sat and stood where Sabari stood. Even if it was only through gestures, the fact that they were communicating with another human being was invigorating for both of them. A single thought consumed them every night: How would they cross the barbed-wire fence and evade the sharp-teethed cages set up by the guards?

One day, nobody knew why, but the guards were not on duty. There were no sharp objects fencing the gateways either. Sabari and the new mother in the camp were the only two with functioning brains who realized that the security personnel were missing. As they fled with the newborn, the skies seemed to open up, as if celebrating their escape with them. Every time they hoisted themselves up, the rain washed away all the sticky mud on them.

The rain lashed hard and for so long, it cast a gloom. One could not tell when day ended and when night began. The mother did not realize when the baby had slipped from her hands, Sabari could not remember when and how she had parted from the mother—everyone was on their own journey. Sabari's long-held desire to escape the camp gave her the strength to run as fast as she could. Otherwise, it was not a downpour any living creature could have survived. If the sun and the moon could keep track and chronicle the events, they might have shared how many times Sabari was knocked down, yet how she always rose and kept braving the relentless rain for three days straight! But then, the noisy rain could have even outwitted their narration. Who could tell!

By the time the rain abated on the fourth morning, Sabari was barely breathing. She had reached the shore of a river. Had the rain continued any longer, even for a few more minutes, she might have got washed away by the river's currents. She herself would have turned into a river that very moment. As if Akasaraja, the god of the skies, had passed a decree, the clouds drifted apart. Obeying Surya's orders, Akasaraja cleaved a path through the dense, swirly clouds, allowing his chariot to glide effortlessly in the skies. Surya blazed with an ethereal brilliance, his radiant beams dancing on the flowing waters. Nature sprang back to life with every passing minute, opened its eyes to the illuminating chariot's wheels and started to breathe afresh. The sounds of nature breathing in and out were enchanting.

The delicate stirrings of nature, as it slowly awakened in the aftermath of the torrential rain, were utterly mesmerizing. It felt as though the very fabric of the universe had resolved to breathe life into the unconscious Sabari. The ripples in the river, with their gentle strokes, soothed her body. Every now and then, tiny fish leapt from the river's depths and brushed against her feet in a tender, fleeting kiss before plunging back into the water. Two palm leaves, come from nowhere, floated on the water and veiled her body against the harsh sunlight. On their way home from collecting food, the birds made a quick stop by Sabari. They pecked at the fruit they were carrying, causing the juice to spill on to her lips and went back to fetch more food for their offspring.

It was dusk, yet Sabari had not regained consciousness. But the life ebbing out of her was fully restored. The moonbeams turned moonlight into amrutam—the divine nectar—and let it rain gently upon her. All of a sudden and at full tilt, the river's flow grew tranquil. Sabari was drunk on divinity that night. She slept peacefully.

5

While Sabari, following her flight from the camp, traversed an incredible, unmatchable, divine experience as she endured the fatal downpour, Matanga was on an expedition of his own. A week before Kannudu's family began their journey to visit his father, Matanga had met his guru, who had suggested he perform penance. And penance was all that mattered to Matanga until he met Kannudu. It was only after he fell ill that he learned about Kannudu, who helped him recover. Matanga Muni noticed that there was an influx of migrants into the forest. He began conversing with them. The more he spoke to them, the better he understood their reasons to move away from their homes. He could weave one anecdote into another and, armed with his deep sensibility and perspicacity, reach a more profound understanding of what was happening. He felt like he was knocking on the doors of a new realm of jnanam. Building cities after destroying forests, chasing aranyavasis away from their homes, mining the earth—everything was happening in accordance with some strategy, it seemed.

He thought sharing his newfound realizations with his guru, his guiding light, would be a good idea. The maharshi, who had advised Matanga that only penance could liberate him from his untouchability, was at an advanced age. He no longer radiated energy as intensely as he once did. As always, Matanga hoped his guru would embrace him at least this time. Instead, the maharshi made him sit at a distance farther than usual. Without showing his pain at this humiliation, Matanga shared with his guru what he had recently discovered. He elaborated on how the forests, the wild, and every creature in it had bestowed on him the dawn of a new jnanam—a fresh awakening of understanding. After recounting the state's atrocities against the aranyavasis, he put forward his question: 'Going by the actions of the nagariks, we can't call them wise, can we?'

As Matanga shared his thoughts, the Brahmin rishi's face reddened.

'Matanga! You will never become an enlightened one. Not only that, you will also lose whatever knowledge you have earned so far. From now on, no matter how many penances you do, your ajnanam will remain. The state, the cities and the king are gifts of God. God bestowed upon us, the nagariks, such extraordinary boons. The king is considered god on earth. Cities are the oxygen that keeps a state running. Without a state, there is no king. All of civilization's progress depends on how powerful the state—rajyam—is.

'Brahmin rishis like me, who have been doing penance for hundreds of years, have poured all our jnanam into strengthening rajyams. Without us, there's no rajyam, and without the rajyam, we're nothing.

'Seeing the radiance on your face, I hoped you'd realize in what incredible ways our knowledge system enables the rajyam. I granted you permission for penance for this very reason. But look at you! You've discarded all your learnings so far and are going in a direction to gain jnanam that is detrimental to the rajyam. That's not your fault, though. It is because of your birth. It is your jati's fault.

'I accepted you as my disciple hoping to turn you into an enlightened one, and thereby turn the members of your jati into ones who would conform to the rules of the rajyam. I had to persuade all my peers to grant you permission for your penance because I could see the qualities of balance and restraint in you. It was also easy to provoke you against your jati, your people, and make you despise them. I could sway you towards believing that you needed to be liberated from what you were born into.

'Just take a look at yourself, though! You have undone everything you gained until now because of the qualities you've inherited from your jati. All the progress you made has been squandered. If only you'd realized the glory in the expansion of the city in your vicinity, considered it as a grand undertaking, conducted a sacrificial offering for the greater good of humanity and made the aranyavasis look at it in the same way, you'd have at least risen to being a half-Brahmin!

'Since you take the side of the primitives, you can never be extricated now. You don't have to come to me any more. Figure your path out yourself. Also, remember that you're being spared only because of the long association between us as guru–shishya. Otherwise, the warriors of our state would have picked you up as a slave by now.

'Leave immediately, before I change my mind and choose to inform them. When better sense prevails in you, and a day comes when you truly acknowledge that the rajyam and nagarikata are for the larger good, that day, state and society will shower respect on you, even if I'm not around. Until then, you're doomed. Now, leave!'

Matanga had nothing to say. Even if he would have wanted to offer an argument, he knew the words would have fallen on deaf ears. Besides, the maharshi had hardly given him a chance to speak. It would be wise to leave the spot before he changed his mind, Matanga thought.

By the time he returned to the forest, Kannudu was nowhere to be seen. Matanga was initially informed that

Kannudu had left with the rest of his family to bring his father back, and also that all of them had fallen into grave danger. Now and then, news of the latest developments from the city arrived. Ten days later, Matanga got the details: Kannudu's family had been captured and taken as slaves, and each of the members was placed in a separate camp. The news made him restless. He believed it was his dharma to save Kannudu, who had given him a new lease of life. Sabari, the sweet little girl who used to sit on his lap, listening to the stories he shared, and who kept calling him 'Tatha!', was now in a slave camp. The one who once played joyfully, hopping around like a fawn, was now in shackles. He could not bear the thought of her being held captive, so he set out towards the city immediately.

In the city, nobody doubted or stopped Matanga because of his attire. Rolled up deerskin mat under his armpit, beaded chain and water-filled kamandalam in his hand, hair pulled up into a knot at the top of his head, long beard—all these were signs welcome in the city. There were strict orders not to trouble anyone in such garb. Such was the luminance on his face and the serenity in his eyes that anyone and everyone bowed to Matanga respectfully. A few who crossed paths with him ushered him to a tiny green belt hosting ashrams for sages who spent their lives performing sacrificial rituals. He was offered an ashram to stay in too, no questions asked.

For a few days, Matanga stayed low to avoid arousing any apprehension, but the very thought of Sabari in a slave camp continued to make him feel agitated. Informing his caretakers that he would like to look around, he tread every inch of the city. Despite finding the town repulsive, he continued with his exploration. He located the slave camps at the intersection of the city's borders and beyond the barbed wires, where the stench was unbearable. There was no visible entry to the camps. He could not make direct enquiries, because a man with such questions would raise countless suspicions, putting his life in danger.

Matanga returned to his ashram, telling the caretakers he had explored the city to his heart's content. He tried to engage the other munis in conversation.

One fine evening, he asked, 'If you accept your king as god, wouldn't that be blasphemy towards the omniscient power?'

The sages were taken aback. They exchanged astonished looks, casting wary glances at Matanga.

In the night, a sixteen-year-old boy named Kalharudu came to Matanga's quarters and alerted him.

'Oh, the best one among munis! If you don't flee from the city tonight, you'll be taken captive. Stay vigilant and return to where you came from as quickly as possible.'

Matanga could sense trouble in Kalharudu's words. Without another thought, he folded the deerskin, took his beaded chain and kamandalam, and walked out of the ashram and the city quietly.

The city was asleep. Matanga did not hesitate to walk towards the base where the slaves were held. As he approached the camp, the security guards noticed his movements. These guards were specially trained to treat anyone and everyone with distrust, even someone as venerable as a sage. They had no reservations about taking him into custody. For the first time in his life, Matanga experienced what it was like to be a prisoner. He was surrounded by inmates who had lost their minds; some even lacked the consciousness that they were human beings. Matanga witnessed their tormented lives and grew increasingly aware that all of them must have been like him earlier, with functioning senses to enjoy and engage with the world. The realization shook him to the core. He could not fathom how anyone could benefit by torturing fellow humans and what purpose the prisons served. The guards neither enquired about who he was nor interrogated him to determine his motives. All they knew was he had been found where he was not supposed to be, and that was enough for them to arrest him.

Matanga sat down, closed his eyes and started penance as his distress exceeded his tolerance. Was he not an expert in overcoming the miseries of his body and surroundings through meditation? The guards at the prison feared

Matanga as they watched him immersed in relentless meditation for three days. They informed the higher authorities about this mysterious man. All the officials deliberated on the matter and ultimately resolved to bring Matanga to the royal assembly.

Upon first glance, Matanga recognized that the assembly hall was the centre of power, a court. His wrists and ankles were still bound in iron chains. A burly young man dragged him to the court. Instead of feeling humiliated, he was curious about the bizarre manner in which the captives were being treated. There was no expression of fear evident on his face. Looking at his serene demeanour, the court could not convict him straightaway. It continued with its proceedings, asking Matanga countless questions, which he answered with utmost honesty. He was interrogated about his jati, guru, penance, his friendship with the aranyavasis, his search for Kannudu's family in the city, and finally asked why he had felt compelled to flee the city in the middle of the night. Nothing was left out, no details escaped scrutiny.

And then, standing before the king in that well-attended assembly, Matanga repeated the question he had posed the munis in the ashram earlier: 'If you accept your king as god, wouldn't that be blasphemy towards the omniscient power?'

The court was shaken by his question. The king responded with roaring laughter. The royal priest stood up and said, 'He must be a Charvaka or Sravana who doesn't believe in God. Regardless of who he is, he is a tapasi, a penitent. Our guards shared first-hand accounts of his intense penance. His birth as an outcaste must be because of his past life's karma. We can't tell what powers he might possess, the miracles he might be capable of, owing to the penances he has done in this life. It's best if he is exiled from our territory. Beheading a tapasi may bring misfortune upon this rajyam.'

Everyone gathered there exchanged looks of trepidation; some even showed signs of repulsion, driven by the fear of the unknown. The king sank into deep thought. The tranquillity on Matanga's face and the fact that it had not diminished even after three days of starving induced a sense of apprehension in everyone. The king's impulse was to kill the outcaste who doubted his status of divinity, but the thought that such an act could bring suffering upon his rajyam unsettled him. Already, there was concerning news of enemy forces approaching the borders in the north. Killing a tapasi might only add to his troubles.

In the end, the assembly reached a unanimous decision that expulsion from their rajyam was the harshest punishment the muni could receive.

For Matanga, the exile was less of a curse and more of a blessing. After his experiences in the city—witnessing the system of slavery and prisons there first hand—he had longed to leave it and return to the forests. Unfortunately, though, his mission of rescuing Sabari from the slave camp in town would remain unaccomplished.

While Matanga considered the expulsion order as anything but punishment, its execution was barbaric. He was made to stand on a cart. The cart-puller announced from time to time that Matanga was an outcaste, that he performed penance despite being an untouchable, and that he had betrayed their king and their kingdom. Upon hearing this, the public gathered to witness the spectacle. They pelted him with stones. Some spat on him. A few onlookers got up on the cart and thrashed him.

Matanga was aghast at the actions of these nagaravasis, the so-called nagariks, trying every conceivable trick and technique to disgrace and hurt another human. More than pain and ridicule, or hurt or humiliation, his heart was filled with an acute dispiritedness. He felt immense pity for his attackers and, overwhelmed by their predicament, tears streamed down his face. Mistaking the tears for those born of his pain, the authorities inflicted even more violence upon him.

The cart carrying Matanga halted at a border. The cart-puller threw him over the thorny fence and out of the kingdom. All the ignominies he faced in the city had sapped the muni of his strength. He collapsed after taking a few steps.

A torrential downpour began. As the rain lashed Matanga, he regained his senses. He made his way through the pitch dark blindly, stumbling every once in a while. He walked till the rain eased and reached the banks of a river. At first, he did not notice a little girl lying there on the ground, unconscious. Once he did, he threw himself into the task of saving the girl right away, determined to use every ounce of his strength and skill to protect her. And when he recognized she was Sabari, his joy knew no bounds! With unwavering dedication, he served her throughout the day, only resting occasionally.

When Sabari realized Matanga was serving her, she hugged him, exclaiming, 'Tatha!' and broke into tears. After learning from Sabari all that had transpired, Matanga gave up all hopes of meeting Kabari and Kannudu again. His immediate concern was to take the little girl to a faraway place as soon as possible. They set out on a journey. The enslaved children in the camp kept appearing in Sabari's nightmares, while Matanga was haunted by visuals of his fellow prisoners and those who had pelted him with stones.

Those who had assaulted him did not know who he was. All they knew was that he was an untouchable. How could a single fact ignite such intense hatred towards him? What is it about the human nature that breeds such animosity towards another? How can anyone rejoice in inflicting pain upon someone else? Who or what induces such behaviour? One might have argued that the authorities and security guards were the reason behind the inmates' mental instability. But who could be blamed for the insanity of those on the streets? Which were the forces, who were the authorities that drove them to such hysteria? And if a man could find pleasure in tormenting another, what did that say about the path humanity was treading? Didn't they realize that by participating in this frenzy they were not just harming others, but gradually turning themselves into victims of their own hatred? As he recollected the abuses and indignities hurled at him as an untouchable, a realization dawned upon Matanga. Wasn't he part of the same frenzy until a while ago? Hadn't his guru instilled the same madness in him about his birth? He had believed his guru's words and loathed himself, hadn't he? He was on a mission to erase all of his past and be reborn, right? Wasn't his decision to retreat to the forests and undertake penance driven by a deep-seated hatred towards his own jati? So many years he lost to this madness!

This self-inflicted shame deeply troubled Matanga. He was shattered as the truth dawned upon him—that he had, in his own way, treated himself as an untouchable. If he had done this to himself, why would the rest of the world treat him any differently?

'Tatha, let's get going.' Matanga was stuck in his contemplative mood till little Sabari shook his hands.

The more he pondered, the more evident it became. The rajyam had mechanisms to instil such mania in its people. Any hysteria backed by it went unquestioned and unchallenged by its public. He himself was an example of such a conformation! His guru had passed on an affliction to him in the name of jnanam. The company he kept with Sabari's parents and the aranyavasis helped him discard that knowledge. For the first time, Matanga understood that jnanam, sacred as it may be, could be dangerous too.

Sabari would be filled with quite a thrill every time she recalled the journey she made with Matanga to the banks of the Pampa. At the time it had felt like she had emerged out of a dark pit and into a world full of light and fresh air. She could not remember how far and for how many days they walked, or whether and when they rested. The haunting memories of the slave camp clung to her long after her escape. Nothing Matanga said about his inner conflict, his emotional unrest, seemed to reach her.

After settling on the banks of the Pampa, Matanga found solace in recounting his story to anyone who visited or enquired about him. He revealed to Sabari his inner turmoil, the whirlwind of thoughts on jnanam and nagarikata that had gripped him upon his arrival in the forest. Sabari hung on to every word, and in time, those words became etched in her memory, especially his inexplicable, unparalleled experience of reaching the tranquil forests of the Pampa. Even on the day Matanga decided to relinquish his life and take eternal rest, he visited every corner of the forest, lingered by the banks of the Pampa, and savoured the sceneries to his heart's content. For one last time, he shared the story with his companions. His words continued to resonate in Sabari's heart whenever she would recall them.

'The city treated me inhumanely. Clinging on to that reality, nursing my wounds from the stone-pelting—just for being an untouchable—I wondered when the scars inside me would heal. I questioned my ability to start my sadhana again. I arrived in this forest with such overwhelming thoughts. The moment I stepped inside it, I encountered gigantic elephants. My instinctive reaction was fear. Tuskers were not new to me, but these ones seemed like tiny mountains. They moved together in harmony. I can still picture the scene in my mind. I stood frozen, anxious, unsure. But then, the elephants reached out and caressed me softly with their trunks. Sabari squeezed her already shut eyes tighter in fear. For the first time I realized the softness and sensitivity hidden within those trunks. In the next moment, Sabari and I found ourselves in the embrace of the gentle giants. The delicate touch of hundreds of elephants!

'Later, a tusker picked me up and put me on its back. Sabari had all but passed out. Many more gentle giants escorted us. By the time we reached the banks of the Pampa, hundreds of branches grazed against me and creepers coiled all around me. The flowers delicately stroked me before showering us with a myriad scents. Hundreds of birds spread their wings above us and soared, singing sweetly. Not to mention the snakes who snuck out of the foliage to peck me. Scarlett bugs, fireflies and countless insects kissed my hands. The incredible journey through the forest to the banks of the Pampa liberated me from the bonds of life.

'Every creature of the forest joined Sabari and me on our journey, if only for a few steps. Every being greeted me lovingly. I was enraptured. I couldn't tell if it was a dream or happening in reality.

'Amidst such feelings of ecstasy, I caught my first glimpse of the Pampa. After making our way through the dense forest, the sight of pure blue waters filled me with both an uncontainable joy and an unsettling sadness. I wept uncontrollably. From the depths of my being, an anguish—or perhaps a joy—swelled up like a waterfall and merged with the Pampa. The tuskers were silent witnesses to all that passed. The Pampa, too, held back from making any sound. Nature, in its entire being, listened to me, my pain, my sorrow, and my distress. With deep affection, it embraced all my emotions and absorbed them into itself. It observed, in quietude, me—as I traversed my tumultuous feelings, allowing joy and peace to emerge slowly within me. In time, all my sorrows disappeared. The only thing that remained inside me was bliss. Pure, unadulterated bliss. A bliss that transcended the dichotomy of body and soul. A bliss beyond meaning. While I was filled with such elation, the tuskers carried me into the Pampa. The warm embrace of the river waters! It purified my soul. The touch of the waters washed away everything I had learnt, all my jnanam, and enveloped me in profound mercy and love, blessing me with a sense of blissful ajnanam—ignorance. Every being in the river caressed me from head to toe, cleansing me. I can't say how long I remained in the waters of the Pampa, nor when I returned to this world and my consciousness. I had no awareness of it. I wasn't aware of Sabari either.'

6

As Sabari narrated the incidents to Sutapa, Kabanda lost himself in the story yet again. No matter how often it was told, it was a story that left the listeners wanting more. Sabari snapped out of the past and returned to the present, but Sutapa was reluctant to come out of the incredible story.

'Amma, have you been living in the forest since then? You seem to embody the very grandeur of the forest inside you! We're too immersed in city life. You've become a part of this forest.'

Sabari smiled gently, like the leaves of the sacred fig tree rustling. She, too, was unwilling to end this conversation.

'Yes, Sutapa. From that day onwards, our lives became inseparable from the forest. Matanga Muni, too, realized the futility of the desire to undertake penances, pursue jnanam and mingle with nagariks. Under his tutelage, I also pondered deeply about nagarikata, anagarikata, jnanam and ajnanam. I also came to realize that the very nagarikata which nagaravasis and those hungry for power proclaim as something indispensable for humanity, is, in essence, contemptible. As it was my own experiences that helped me gain this deeper understanding, there was no space for doubt. I could comprehend the multitude of ways in which nagarikata separates mankind from nature. The ways of being uncivilized weren't hard to grasp either. I learnt about them and chose to be a part of anagarikata. At every given opportunity, I explain my stance on anagarikata to my fellow folks and visitors, but gently, not in the manner of arguments and debates. I am not a preacher either.

'I advise everyone to befriend nature, hug trees, treat every being as an equal. I recommend a way of life that fosters nothing but love and compassion. Stop this relentless pursuit of the universe's buried secrets. Instead, learn to listen to its whispers. Our existence will find its true meaning if we develop a keen ear for the subtle murmurs of the universe. Our life's ambition must be to recognize and revel in its mysteries, without an urge to unravel them. The universe is here to awe us. After a while, once you overcome being awed, you will witness this cosmic play in an impersonal, passionless way, only to become a part of it. This is the act of intimately fusing with the light of ajnanam. I'm encouraging you to immerse yourself in the sadhana of such ajnanam.

'Jnanam has been distancing us—from nature, from all other beings in it, and from life itself. It has estranged us from the universe. The journey that nagariks undertake in the name of jnanam is creating havoc on humans. Religions, kingdoms, caste hierarchies, hostilities, wars, massacres, the chasm between touchables and untouchables, the unsatiated desire for winning—all these are consequences of civilization, knowledge and science. Mankind is currently entrapped by what it has created. Its infatuation with nature is fuelled by an intense greed, which has been spreading like wildfire in people's hearts. The paths to satisfying this greed—what's known as knowledge and science—are worshipped. I reject such jnanam and advocate ajnanam instead. I ask you to see the resplendence of ignorance. You lot equate ajnanam with darkness, but I consider it to be light.

'The nagariks believe that man is the mightiest of all creatures, the master of all species. I don't accept that. When you realize there's no one ruler, it would be easier to acknowledge that every being in this universe is the master of its own life. Each life is special in itself and has its own way of living. Only such understanding can lead to greater good. Nagarikata has made you forget the original sequence—observe, marvel, understand, respect, love. A new order has emerged in its place—observe, loathe, ridicule, attack, control.'

Sutapa could not grasp the full essence of Sabari's words. Nevertheless, he listened attentively. Kabanda interrupted their conversation, asking the weary Sabari to get some rest.

Sabari walked out of the ashram. The kadimi trees outside looked like another ashram. She stood like a tree among those trees. Emptying her conscious mind of everything that she had recollected and shared, she could stand still, experiencing only the breeze.

In the meantime, Sutapa sauntered along the banks of the Pampa and Kabanda left the ashram to gather some fruits.

Day stepped into evening, gently melting into its soft embrace. The whole forest was getting ready to enjoy that part of the day. The sky and earth were changing colours in joy. Shadows talked over whether they ought to stop playing the game of short and long. Sounds and silences were making their presence felt after occasional intervals of stillness. An amiable contest started between light and darkness. Every being in the forest was experiencing and becoming a part of the continuous flow of time, ever new and ever fresh, every day.

Sutapa watched the sunrise of the following morning with rapture. The path to the Pampa was lit, sunbeams scattered throughout, glistening in myriad hues.

As he bathed in the Pampa, Sutapa remembered Sabari's question: 'Son, would you be returning to Ayodhya?' He had said he would. The breathtaking beauty of the forests and the mesmerizing experiences he had had there were not enough to make him forget his city. He fondly remembered his parents, siblings, friends and peers back home. He had a strong desire to soon end his journey, return home, and share with them stories of all the new places he had seen, the new experiences he had had.

He did not have the same passionate relationship with forests as Sabari did. All his bonds were with humans. Nature was outside him, there was a distance between them. Indeed, nature gave him joy, but he could not tell whether he instilled in her a similar emotion. He watched her as a distinct presence, with fear, joy, wonder and apprehension.

In contrast, Kabanda seemed one with nature. He knew only joy, no agitations or dilemmas. It was the same with Sabari. Both of them are blessed to be so. I could never be like them, Sutapa thought.

After finishing his bath, Sutapa wandered in the forest for a while before returning to Sabari's abode.

He now observed the abode intently. The day before, too exhausted from his journey, Sutapa had longed for a place to rest, free from any fear of danger. He had stayed back at the ashram for the day. Today, he set out at dawn and returned only when morning was in its full glory.

He now understood what made Matanga's home special. Four trees stood as four pillars of the structure. Branches and boughs served as its roofs, while leaves and creepers formed its walls. So verdant the latter were that the walls seemed to be covered in a dense blanket of green. For ventilation, the twigs had been broken in various places, the hollowed-out parts shaped like animals. Except for that one thing: there didn't seem to be any traces of human intervention in the construction of the place.

While Sutapa was keenly examining every inch of the dwelling, which could easily host up to ten people, he heard a sound—someone was coming. He turned around to see who it was and was shell-shocked. Were they men who looked like monkeys or monkeys that looked like men?

'We've come here to meet Maharshi Sabari,' said one of them. 'I'm Hanuma,' he continued. 'Please inform Sabari Mata that our king Sugreeva is also here.'

Sutapa involuntarily bowed in respect to Hanuma, the one with the muscular body and serene voice.

'I too am a guest in this ashram,' Sutapa replied. 'It seems like Sabari Mata hasn't returned from the banks of the Pampa yet.'

Hanuma walked away; Sutapa followed him. Along with Sugreeva, all three of them settled on a towering mound of stones lying over a massive stretch of green.

Hanuma asked Sutapa, 'Who are you? Where did you come from?' Sutapa answered, 'I came here from the north, driven by wanderlust.'

A short while later, Sabari and Kabanda arrived and warmly greeted Hanuma and Sugreeva.

'Have you settled well on the Rushyamuka mountain?' Sabari asked. Sugreeva answered this question with a lowered gaze. Hanuma picked up the conversation. 'It's not that the Rushyamuka mountain is lacking in anything, Amma, but our hearts are ablaze with all the dishonour we suffered. We're unable to put out those fires.'

'Such is the aspiration for rajyam, Hanuma. Those flames can never be extinguished. Do you think Vali is at peace? He's always anxious about you both, carrying within him a deep sense of insecurity. Why don't you forget Vali and his kingdom and live peacefully on the mountain?'

Hanuma looked at Sugreeva, who was fuming.

'We can, Amma.' It was Sugreeva who spoke. 'We're already on the mountain. But I doubt my brother would make peace with it. Vali has not only seized my share of the rajyam but has also driven me out, fearing that I might harm him. He's far too powerful for me to challenge in a duel. I'm living like a destitute on the mountains and taking shelter under trees. In my heart, there is a deep restlessness. I'm unable to find a way out of this.'

Kabanda smiled gently. 'Only yesterday this new guest of ours told us about a great man. At his parents' request, he relinquished his rajyam to his brother and, clad in the plainest of attires, went on to live in the forests with his wife and brother. We were pleased to hear about this venerable individual and his story. Your only way out is to realize that peace lies in giving up your throne and power. Where else can you find peace if not within?'

'Did he abandon his throne to live in the forests? Or did he lose it in a war?'

'There was no war to begin with. It seems he left his rajyam at his father's behest.'

Hanuma and Sugreeva looked at each other in surprise.

'Where are they now?'

'They also seem to be travelling towards the south.'

'Maybe they aren't capable enough?' Sugreeva wagered a guess. Sutapa responded to these words at once:

'It is said that even gods can't withstand our Ramachandra's valour. No, it's not mere rhetoric. It is true. Our Ramachandra had broken Siva's bow to win Sitadevi as his wife during her svayamvara. He was trained in warfare by Vishwamitra, a royal sage. When he used to practise archery every morning in Ayodhya, the sound of him pulling the string of his bow to shoot an arrow would reverberate through the entire city. Foes either chose to flee or surrendered on seeing Ramachandra, the one with strong shoulders and a radiant face. He was only too obedient to his father, but is not someone without courage.'

The very mention of Ramachandra caused a flood of emotion to course through Sutapa. His words had everyone around him spellbound. All four present had the desire to see Rama.

Sabari was the first to break the spell. 'Sugreeva! I can't put out the flaming desire for rajyam in you. Maybe Rama can give you some advice on this matter. Wait for his arrival.' Addressing Hanuma, she continued: 'Son, Hanuma! You're a wise one. I know you have clarity and strength of mind. Your words, full of prudence, hold a special place in my heart. But today, I'm too tired to get into a conversation with you.'

'For some reason, I'm beginning to trust Rama,' Kabanda said to Hanuma. 'I have goosebumps just thinking about how he could relinquish his rajyam as if it were nothing. You, too, put your trust in him! Your wisdom and his benevolence would make a fine combination. If you ever come across Rama in your life, don't leave his side. Now you know what even I feel about rajyam. When you meet him, do share my thoughts with Rama just as Sabari would.'

Hanuma and Sugreeva invited Sutapa to Rushyamuka.

Hanuma admired Rama's sacrifice and Sugreeva his valour. Both were keen to learn more about him. Sutapa told them that he would like to spend a few more days in Matanga Muni's ashram and by the banks of the Pampa. Once he left this place, he would visit them in Rushyamuka.

Sugreeva had approached Sabari hoping the aranyavasis would support him and declare Vali as their enemy. But it was evident that she would not permit such a thing. Her words suggested that he live on Rushyamuka forever. But how could he live tolerating the adharma that had been meted out to him? He posed this question to Sabari.

'What is dharma, Sugreeva?' Despite the tenderness in Sabari's voice, the question cut him deep.

Sugreeva lost his composure. He was feeble-minded and short-tempered. Those who believe they are in unfortunate and undeserving circumstances are quick to flare up. Sugreeva was in a similar state of mind, unable to find a way out of his predicament. His immense anger towards Vali could be manoeuvred in any direction without effort. That he respected Sabari, there was no doubt, but given that his very life was in danger, Sugreeva felt she was ridiculing his plight by raising an unnecessary debate about dharma. Sabari noticed his irritation.

'Sugreeva! I'm asking about the dharma of nature and the dharma of every living being. Not the rajya dharma that Vali is abiding by. You feel animosity towards Vali, but you're not the least bit critical of rajya dharma. You both intend to create a kingdom out of all the aranyavasis and are trying hard to establish dharma anew or bring in a new dharma altogether. These ambitions may be enticing to you but are repulsive to us. We're worlds apart on this topic. I'm happy to share my thoughts on the matter and listen to yours, but what can I do if you're irked by them? You can only engage in a war of words with me.' She smiled gently.

'You're still stuck in your anagarik ways, Amma. Nagarikata is spreading its wings. If we can't catch it now, we won't be able to continue on this earth.'

'Have we not survived for as long as we have? All right, let's assume for a second we won't survive any longer. But what does the universe lose if we don't exist?'

Sugreeva stood up and bowed to Sabari in reverence.

It was Hanuma who responded to Sabari: 'No matter how much we try to engage with each other, all our conversations will inevitably lead to this unanswerable question. In times when humans, backed by nagarikata, are strongly questioning the need for the universe if not for our existence; in times when they consider themselves masters of the earth, next only to god; in times when "king is god" has become an axiom; in times when people yearn for a stable rajyam; in times when the prevailing belief is that not only can nagarikata help cities grow but, in turn, it can save the human race—your question of "But what does the universe lose if we don't exist?" seems as futile and meaningless as someone weeping alone in a forest expecting solace. There is no answer to your question. Nagarikata is the quest for answers to nature's mysteries; it isn't being content with unresolved questions.'

That said, he bowed to Sabari and took her leave.

Sugreeva and Hanuma went back the way they had come. Sutapa found the whole conversation quite peculiar. He feared the suggestion that there would be no loss to the universe even if humans became extinct. He shuddered at the very thought of a world without humans.

Do these elders really want to see the end of the human race? How shocking! For people who come across as epitomes of serenity and love, aren't these two, Sabari and Kabanda, nurturing destructive thoughts within them?

Sutapa wanted to leave immediately and join the other two visitors at the Rushyamuka mountain. Sabari was quick to catch the change in Sutapa's facial expression and felt pity for him. She could understand his reasons for feeling uncertain.

'Sutapa! Fear not,' Sabari said in a reassuring tone. 'The intention behind my words is not what you assume. You shall slowly realize that … You may stay here without any worry for a few more days,' she added, and went inside.

That Sabari could read his mind unsettled Sutapa. Her uncanny ability of sensing his fear even when he had not uttered a word about it terrified him even more. The first step of nagarikata, he realized, was fear—a truth he had yet to acknowledge. Born in a city, he had been plagued by many a fear since his birth, and over time, they became his constant companions. The very idea of living without dread had never occurred to him. But his travels through the forests introduced him to a new sport: that of overcoming his fears. Though they were home to numerous frightening experiences, he revelled in the beauty of the forests. Each time he discovered there was no reason to be afraid, he felt a profound satisfaction. His journey through the woods grew into a quest for more of that contentment.

But now, a new fear gripped him: the powers that Sabari and Kabanda possessed—forces he could neither quite understand nor control. He decided to leave the ashram within the next two days. The invitation from Sugreeva and Hanuma, who seemed anything but ordinary, was tempting. They may have appeared different in their looks and innate dispositions, but both seemed to share the same outlook. Sutapa was eager to witness their contrasting lives from up close.

There was one thing that Sutapa realized during his journey: it was diversity. In his expansive trek from the north to the south, he encountered a wide array of living beings. When he was in Ayodhya, he had not known how diverse the human race was, let alone the variety of animals, trees and insects that existed. He was a weaver, a family occupation passed down over generations, now run by his father, brothers and relatives. The women of his household, too, participated in the weaving activities after finishing their domestic chores. Unlike his elders, who adored their profession, Sutapa's heart had never been in it, and he carried out the tasks assigned to him more out of a sense of obligation than out of passion.

Sutapa had always been fond of travelling, ever since boyhood. His favourite pastime was leaving the house for a day and spending time in the neighbouring villages, fields or gardens. He was keen on making new friends. In the beginning, his family struggled to come to terms with his wanderlust. Fearing that one day he might not return home from his expeditions, they started to track his every movement and put in place several restrictions to restrain him. They only entrusted him with errands that did not require him to step out of the house. Anyone who was friendly with him was looked at with suspicion and was bothered with one too many questions.

They did not realize that the more they restricted him, the greater his love for travel grew. Sutapa learned tricks to disappear from home for a couple of days without leaving behind a single trace about his whereabouts. He had no teachers; only his surroundings and experiences to learn from. His family married him off at an early age and, soon after, he became a father to two children. These additional responsibilities failed to bring about any change in Sutapa's nature—except, with age, he took a keen interest in recounting to others the wonders he had witnessed during his travels. Sutapa's family was now convinced that no matter how far he went, he would return home to share his discoveries with them. They stopped bothering him. In time, everyone took interest in the stories he would tell. His wife, too, enjoyed his gift for storytelling. After a while, Sutapa's wanderlust took him beyond the Sarayu river.

Those were the days when news of Ramachandra's coronation had spread far and wide. It was a long-awaited event. It was no secret that Maharaja Dasharatha, having grown too old to rule, intended to retire and pass the throne on to his eldest son. Public opinion was that each of Dasharatha's sons was a gem, but Ramachandra was the best among them. He was dark-complexioned, and to the common folk that led to the impression that he was one of them. He stood tall and was well built, his body a testament to years of rigorous training and discipline. His sharp features added to his commanding presence. He seldom appeared in public, and that set him apart from any other prince. People thronged to the streets to catch a glimpse of him when, along with his three brothers, he made a rare public appearance. They hoped that this prince, Ramachandra, would be their king soon. When the news of his coronation broke, the festivities began without delay. But even before the festivities could come into full swing, news of the coronation being cancelled spread like wildfire. It was clear that it had not been postponed because of unfavourable circumstances but been truly cancelled. The Ayodhyavasis were utterly dumbfounded when they found out that Ramachandra would go into exile, to live in forests, instead of becoming a king, as per Dasharatha's orders.

When Sabari had asked him, Sutapa had not revealed the real reason behind Ramachandra's abdication, but he knew a thing or two about what had unfolded in the inner chambers of the palace on the eve of the coronation. He had not been able to comprehend the matter in full, but whatever he could, had been hard for him to digest. Ignoring what he could not grasp, he left Ayodhya and followed Ramachandra into the forests hoping to find out more.

As soon as the news of Ramachandra's coronation broke out, anyone associated with the capital city for their livelihood was inundated with tasks tied to the occasion. With not a moment to spare, they were wholly immersed in making arrangements for the sacred rites and countless celebrations.

Being one of the few families of weavers responsible for preparing the clothes for the royal household and priests, they had been working relentlessly. Even Sutapa's extended family, including his paternal uncles, burned the midnight oil. After all, even new clothes for Vasishtha, the royal priest, was their responsibility. The skilled weavers got the garments ready in no time.

With the coronation ceremony only two days away, Sutapa arranged all the delicate garments in a beautiful basket and reached the royal city with his elder brother. It was a memorable day for him. The place where they had to deliver the clothes warranted a long walk from the city's entrance. Sutapa, consumed by wanderlust, did not mind the long walk at all. The weight of the clothes on his head did not bother him. His walk exuded enthusiasm. However, his brother was already panting to keep up with Sutapa's speed. It was as if his feet were indeed made of lotuses, mirroring the meaning of his very name, 'Padmapada'. The basket he was carrying slowed him down. None of his ploys to escape this errand had succeeded, and here he was, on foot and carrying heavy baggage. The streets of the royal city, its people, horses, palanquins and flower shops failed to appeal to him as they did to Sutapa. After a while, Padmapada stopped under the shade of a tree, putting the bags down next to him. Sutapa was forced to join his brother. Both the brothers wiped the sweat off their foreheads with their turbans. They drank the cold water they carried with them.

Sutapa could not take his eyes off the royal city, whereas Padmapada had his eyes trained on the ground while he rested.

'Anna, look how beautiful the royal city is!' said Sutapa.

'If people are slogging away to arrange everything, anything can be beautiful. Who knows how many like us toiled to make it look this gorgeous,' said Padmapada, dismissing Sutapa's point.

Sutapa was shocked at his brother's words. He had never heard such a thing.

'What toiling are you talking about, Anna? One must be blessed to work for the royal city and those who live there!'

'It's not a blessing, it's a misfortune. In other words, it's our karma,' Padmapada said, clearly agitated.

His brother's words were beyond Sutapa. He could have argued with him but only if he would have understood what was being said. Did his brother utter these words because he was exhausted from walking in the sun and carrying a heavy bundle of clothes? But it was not like his anna was unused to such things. Maybe the sun was a bit harsher than usual, and the baggage heavier. But still, so what? Was his brother losing his mind? Sutapa feared the worst for a moment.

Maharaja Dasharatha, his queens, Kaushalya, Sumitra and Kaikeyi, his sons, Ramachandra, Lakshmana, Bharata and Shatrughna, and their wives, Sita, Urmila, Mandavi and Shrutakeerti—their very names gave him goosebumps.

To top it all, Sri Ramachandra was deeply adored by every Ayodhyavasi! The city was abuzz with anticipation of his coronation, and whispers of his future reign promised that dharma would flourish under his just rule, it would walk on all of its four feet. On such an auspicious occasion, was it one's fortune or misfortune to be entrusted with important duties? Sutapa was not pleased with Padmapada's stance.

'This is our good fortune, Anna! It's Ramachandra's coronation. He will become Raja Rama. We're working towards such a great cause. It must be a result of the punya we earned in our previous lives.'

Padmapada lifted his head slowly, looked at Sutapa with pity and sighed deeply.

'How does it matter who becomes the king? What difference would it make? If Ramachandra takes over the throne, tell me one good change that would happen in *our* lives.'

Sutapa was flustered.

'Ramachandra is the most capable one of them all. Maharaja Dasharatha is too old to rule now. Ramachandra can protect us from the enemy rajyams, prevent them from encroaching on our land. He can save us from misery. Isn't that enough?'

'Name one of our enemy kingdoms.'

'I don't know…'

'Let's say another king took over this rajyam instead of Ramachandra, wouldn't you serve the new king? Wouldn't you weave clothes for him?'

Sutapa was now sure that his brother had lost his mind, and he grew a little frightened. Convinced that their conversation was going nowhere, he put the basket atop his head and resumed walking.

The city was in a festive mood. There was joy everywhere except on Padmapada's face.

Suddenly, the royal guards instructed passers-by to step aside and clear the way. They ordered everyone to remain still, cordoning off the public on either side of the street.

It was clear to all why such an arrangement had been imposed—someone important from the palace was about to pass through the streets. Sutapa's excitement knew no bounds. 'Who knows, if we're lucky, we might even catch a glimpse of Ramachandra!'

Unable to contain his curiosity, Sutapa asked the guard before him, who confirmed his hopes. Moments later, Ramachandra's chariot entered the street.

Every pore in Sutapa's body seemed to transform into an eye. How handsome the prince was! He was surprised to find a man's handsomeness so captivating. Ramachandra's speciality was that he was gentle and mighty at one and the same time. His face was radiant, with a deep, rich complexion. His eyes were as white as lotuses, shoulders broad, and arms long. He gleamed in a light green robe, a tiny crown resting atop his head, and only a neckpiece or two adorning his form.

The beautiful sight passed too soon. Sutapa looked at his brother, who was gazing down at the street.

'Anna! Did you see Ramachandra?'

'No. Let's go.'

Everyone was allowed to move again, and the street regained its ebullience.

'Anna! Tell me honestly. Weren't you delighted to see Ramachandra? Earlier you scared me with your words and now I'm frightened by your indifference,' Sutapa said.

'If you'd like to eliminate this fear, you must meet Charvaka. Tell me if you're interested, and I'll take you to him. He knows every secret this world contains.'

Whoever he was, Sutapa was sure he did not want to meet him. By the time they returned home after completing their work in the city, it was past the hour for dinner. Sutapa finished his meal and dozed off for a few hours before his father assigned him a fresh set of errands. This time, his brother would not accompany him, and the bundle of clothes was smaller.

Following the previous day's exchanges and the anxiety that they had led to, Sutapa felt relieved that his brother was not going to join him.

That evening, Sutapa went to Vasishtha's quarters to hand over freshly woven clothes for him. Just as he was about to knock on the door, he heard a woman's voice. 'Aiyo, what a calamity this is!' said the woman.

Sutapa had seen Vasishtha only on a few occasions earlier. As for the woman, he could not make out who she was nor guess why she was wailing. In any case, he left the pile of clothes he had brought on a wooden table and was about to leave when he heard her say—

'Sri Ramachandra is dear to me, even more so than Bharata. I can't imagine harming him in any way. And why should I? Why did you choose me for this task? Can't you ask Sumitra or Kaushalya to do it for you? I simply cannot do what you're asking me to. Sri Ramachandra is dearer than life to me. He must be coronated, and we all must celebrate it grandly.'

Sutapa still could not figure out who she was!

'Amma, Kaikeyi!' Vasishtha addressed her in a severe tone. Sutapa's heart leapt out of his chest.

Except knowing that Maharaja Dasharatha's third wife was Kaikeyi, Sutapa, as a commoner, had never had a chance to see her. But even before the desire to catch sight of her could emerge within him fully, his legs began to tremble as he heard the maharshi's next words.

'Rama's coronation will only harm us, Kaikeyi! You queens don't fully understand what happened at Sri Rama's wedding. The moment the ferocious Parashurama began unleashing his wrath on Rama, you all fled to your chambers. I was the one who pacified him. I restored the friendship between the Raghu dynasty and Jamadagni's son Parashurama. I'm bound to keep my word to him.'

'What word? What right do you have to promise anyone that you'll send Rama to the forest?' The unbridled fury in Kaikeyi's tone was unmistakable.

Her questions caused vexation to lace the gravity in Vasishtha's tone.

'Are you asking me to assert my authority? Kaikeyi! I'm upholding the values of the Raghu clan and ruling over your rajyam through your king. Without my command, Dasharatha doesn't go ahead with even a minor task, because he's incapable of doing so. You're well aware of the fact that it is I who establish all dharmas, decide who is assigned which duty across this rajyam, and ensure it's carried out! Yet you question me? Perhaps you're forgetting your limits, living in the midst of all the extravagance you get to enjoy. You will be destroyed were you to choose to revolt against me.'

Kaikeyi cried out. The shriek, filled with dread, was so sudden and loud that Sutapa trembled.

'Please save our rajyam, Maharshi,' she said shakily.

'I called you here with that very intention. Sri Rama's marriage was possible only because of my generosity. Otherwise, a war would have broken out that day. Parashurama's hatred for the Kshatriyas is no secret. You are well aware of how many kings and emperors he has killed! I was the one who saved Rama from him and his weapon. I was the one who made the deal!'

'What deal?'

'Before Rama is crowned, he must spread Arya dharma across the southern region. I made a promise to Parashurama. Only after Rama fulfils this duty will he be coronated as king. Parashurama's sole ambition in life is the widespread adoption of Arya dharma backed by Brahmins. He has chosen Rama as his means. Rama must bring the territories and the Dasyas—the natives south of the Vindhyas—into our dominion. For that, he has to go into the forests.'

Kaikeyi took a considerable amount of time to let Vasishtha's words sink in. Meanwhile, Sutapa was so terrified that he was drenched in sweat.

Finally, Kaikeyi spoke:

'One could simply declare a war against the southern dominions and overpower them. Didn't Maharshi Vishwamitra seek Rama's and Lakshmana's help to defeat the Dasyas? As a prince, Rama can fight these wars and return for his coronation. Why should I demand two boons from Maharaja Dasharatha when such a straightforward strategy could work? Why should I insist he send Rama to the forest and coronate Bharata instead? Why go through such a trial? Why take such a serpentine route? Why make me the sacrificial goat?'

As the true nature of their conversation became clear, Sutapa shoved a part of his upper garment into his mouth to stop himself from screaming.

Vasishtha calmed down a bit and elaborated further on the topic:

'What do you think of the southern region? Who do you think the Dasyas are? Earlier, Rama killed a careless Dasya rani, Tataki. But now, his task will need to be different. Killing them won't do. They have too many warriors. Unlike us, they don't have kingdoms and power structures, and neither do they follow any dharma. They have no idea about what it means to be civilized; they are full of ignorance. But there's unimaginable wealth present in their forests. Rama must live in these forests to bring them into our fold of dharma and their riches under our control. He has to make them passionate about nagarikata and the Arya dharma. He must befriend the people of the forests. He must make them believe that he is a divine incarnation—an avatara purusha. Wherever he sets foot, he must leave his mark and propagate the benefits of adopting Arya dharma. I'm not ruling out the possibility of a war. But it must be fought among themselves without any trouble to the soldiers and inhabitants of Ayodhya. They'll have to shed their own blood to make us victorious. We devised this tactic with Parashurama, and you are merely one of the means to the end. There's no escape for you. If you don't obey my command, your rajyam will collapse. Now, don't waste my time with your futile arguments, and better return to your inner chambers.'

Vasishtha's blunt tone said it all. Their conversation was over. Kaikeyi struggled to hold back her tears and stood up, trying to muster courage.

'Kaikeyi! You are doing this. You are doing this by yourself. You are doing this out of love and affection towards your son. You are doing this to become Queen Mother. I dare you to disclose to anyone my role in all this! And don't you worry about getting the blame. You shall remain in the annals of history. Don't yield because of Dasharatha's sorrow or entreaties. Trust me when I say the plan is to uplift the Raghu dynasty and Rama. Rest assured, good things will follow. Now, leave.'

Sutapa stood still like a rock. Kaikeyi and her maid Manthara rushed out, too engrossed in their thoughts to notice him.

Sutapa somehow pulled himself out of the shock and walked home in a daze, as if all the life had drained out of him. He could not contain the intense anguish and fury that came over him as he witnessed the preparations for the big event, both at home and on the streets. His emotions were on the verge of spilling over. 'Listen to me! What will happen tomorrow is…' he wanted to scream his lungs out. But his lips would not part—he remembered Vasishtha's ultimatum to Kaikeyi. For the first time in his life, Sutapa realized how agonizing it was to guard a secret.

While Sutapa was struggling to bury the secret deep within himself, rumours spread like wildfire in Ayodhya. Not a soul spared Kaikeyi from their curses. They condemned Manthara too. As their entry into the capital city was restricted, everyone did their best to add to the ferment, trying to pass along the gossip about the pair's cunning plan. Sutapa had no choice but to remain silent despite knowing the truth. He was deeply saddened by everything he heard. But not for long. Soon, the news arrived officially, albeit in snippets.

'Rama was called by Dasharatha to his chamber.'

'Rama has agreed to comply with all of Dasharatha's orders. He has promised his stepmother that he will leave for the forests soon.'

'Dasharatha fainted.'

'Kaushalya is inconsolable.'

'As soon as news of Rama's exile broke, Sita announced that she'd follow her husband into the forests. She's disregarding Rama's objections.'

'Rama pacified the enraged Lakshmana.'

'Now Lakshmana is insisting that he too will join his brother.'

'Rama and Lakshmana, accompanied by Sita, have started their journey to the forest.'

'Sita is still wearing some of her jewellery, but Rama and Lakshmana are without any adornments, dressed in plain clothes, like ascetics. They have tied their hair up into knots on the top of their heads. But they did not leave behind their bows and arrows.'

'Look, they are leaving Ayodhya!'

'Come, come, let's go and take a look.'

'Why simply watch them? Let's follow them for a while.'

'Why only a while? Let's bid them goodbye at the banks of the river.'

'Why bid them goodbye? Let's join them. What's left in the city without Rama? Can't we survive on fruits, vegetables and leaves? Isn't the jungle better than a land bereft of dharma?'…

The emotions of the public were soaring. Sutapa was one among the many who followed Ramachandra into the woods. After crossing the Sarayu river, Ramachandra dissuaded them from continuing any further. Some returned to Ayodhya, some set off in different directions in the jungle itself. Sutapa got separated from one such party of explorers and ended up near the banks of the Pampa.

Sutapa was utterly amazed at the prospects life was throwing at him. His chance meeting with Sabari made him realize the intention behind Vasishtha's plans. Ramachandra may have travelled to the south to proliferate Arya dharma, but it would also help him expand the dominion of Ayodhya, Sutapa thought. After listening to Sabari's life story, he simultaneously loved and feared the rajyam. He firmly believed that if not for the state and cities, people would not survive. Villages, too, survived under the protection and vigilance of towns. But that night, he was equally troubled by the idea that cities could expand only at the expense of forests and their creatures. However, there was no way that cities would stay away from forests. Sutapa's fears stemmed from putting together two things: Ramachandra's travelling south and Vasishtha's strategy. Hanuma and Sugreeva's arrival this morning showed him how aggravated the situation had become. Rajyams, rivalry between siblings over them, and resorting to violence for the same seemed to be commonplace. Was Ramachandra going to sort all this out in accordance with Arya dharma?

All these thoughts made Sutapa's head throb. He had never been this restless during his time in the forests. Sabari's ashram, which had initially felt like a peaceful abode, now appeared to be a war zone with two opposing dharmas. He decided to leave the ashram as soon as he could. For quite a while he had forgotten what had made him set out on this journey—which was to observe everything that would come his way. His goal was to visit places. He gazed at the hills and waterfalls through the day, basked in the tranquillity of their sounds, and returned to the ashram at dusk to rest for the night.

Sutapa decided to leave Sabari's ashram for the Rushyamuka mountain and, from there, continue his journey towards the sea. He promised to visit Sabari and Kabanda on his way back. Sabari shared with Sutapa all the hopes she had pinned on Rama.

'It's not an ordinary feat, your Rama abandoning the throne. He appears to have no real interest in rajyam. If he ever comes here, I'd like to ask him to disseminate my ideas and teachings in the cities. If there's even a single Arya warrior who can understand my perspective, I hope that together we can prevent further damage. I hope Rama decides to visit the sea like you.' Sabari smiled to herself at such wishful thinking.

Sutapa was certain that nothing Sabari was hoping for would happen. Ramachandra and Sabari are poles apart, he concluded. Sutapa also knew that Ramachandra would undoubtedly come to the edge of the southern region where Sabari's ashram was. He shared this with Sabari, to her delight.

'Ramachandra is keen on visiting the seas of the south, Amma. He will come for sure. I can't guarantee that he will follow the same route I did to arrive at this ashram, but I'm sure he won't head back to Ayodhya without going to the sea.'

Sabari was thrilled at his words. Her hope, faint until then, started to flicker brighter. She looked at Kabanda.

'Kabanda! You must bring Sri Rama to our ashram now. I'm entrusting you with this task. It may be true that one can go further south without necessarily touching the Pampa, but no one can miss the crossroads at which these paths diverge. Please go to the junction immediately and stay put. When Rama and Lakshmana arrive there, invite them to our ashram on my behalf. If it wasn't for my age, I'd have gone to the crossroads myself and waited for him.

But I'm just too exhausted. I'm like a ripe fruit that may fall off the tree any moment. However, I wouldn't wish to die without seeing Rama, without telling him the story of Matanga Muni, and without educating him about how the rajyam encroaches upon and demolishes the earth, its sons and daughters and nature entirely. That's why you have to start right away. Be there at the crossroads … Aiyo! What if they have already gone past the—'

Observing the anxiety and disquiet on Sabari's face, Sutapa felt sorry for her. He knew that her wish would not come true.

As for Kabanda, he was hesitant to leave Sabari alone in the state she was in but could not disregard her request. He, too, desired to meet Sri Rama and have a discussion with him. Though he could not speak as wisely as Sabari could, Kabanda was no less erudite. If, for some reason, Rama denied his request to visit the ashram, Kabanda could relay Sabari's arguments to him effectively. There was no one else in the forest who could do this.

Sabari repeatedly warned Kabanda not to move from his post at the crossroads. Despite his reluctance to leave the ashram, Kabanda took leave of Sabari, asking her to take care of herself, and left with Sutapa. He also hoped that he could do some good by guiding Sutapa to his next destination.

Sabari was at peace knowing Kabanda would accomplish what he had set out for. From Sutapa's words, she could gather that Rama would be able to advocate and realize her vision and ideals well. Her only wish was to meet him before she died and, through him, spread her philosophy. If that happened, she could die without a worry. From that moment on, Sabari was consumed by thoughts of meeting Rama.

She splashed water from the Pampa on her eyes, heavy from the weariness of waiting for Rama, and then fixed her gaze till as far as it would go. Her waiting was her meditation.

7

Riddled with grief and rage over his wife's abduction, Rama continued to journey through the forest. Lakshmana, too, seethed no less inside, but he could not show it as he was also responsible for safeguarding his brother every minute of the day. They had crossed jungles, rivers, hills. They had absolutely no idea about where they were headed except that they were moving towards the south.

One day, Kabanda came across the brothers. He recognized them at first glance, even from a distance. Sutapa's descriptions of the two had been elaborate enough for their appearances to be engraved in his mind. Not being able to contain himself, Kabanda quickened his pace and almost sprinted towards them. The haste with which he approached the brothers immediately put them on alert. They aimed their weapons at him. While Rama's arrows injured Kabanda's hands, Lakshmana's targeted his eyes.

Kabanda collapsed to the ground. While for a moment he did doubt whether they were truly the venerable Rama and Lakshmana whom Sutapa had spoken so highly of, Kabanda was quickly swept by an all-encompassing compassion for the men who had attacked him without so much as asking him why he had approached them.

The brothers moved towards Kabanda cautiously and asked, 'Who are you? Why were you charging at us?'

'No, no. I wasn't charging at you, I was only approaching you. I thought you were Rama and Lakshmana and rushed towards you.'

Kabanda, grievously injured and worn out, felt a deep sense of disappointment. And yet, he summoned the strength to sit up.

'Sutapa, an Ayodhyavasi, told us about you. Our mother Sabari has been anticipating your arrival at the ashram more than me. I camped here in the middle of the forest to take you there. Why did you attack me? I didn't do you any harm, did I?'

For a while, Rama and Lakshmana had no answers.

'We assumed you were rushing towards us with ill intentions. Also, your gaze was fixed on us. Those were reasons enough for us to suspect you. We're already in great distress, constantly under threat. To survive in this forest, we must remain distrustful and vigilant at all times. That's why we didn't think twice before attacking you.

By the way, what does Sabari Mata, or even you, have to do with us…?'

Rama and Lakshmana continued with their barrage of questions, but Kabanda, now fading, struggled to keep up with them as he bled profusely. His distress was palpable, and with each passing moment it seemed as though he might lose consciousness from the heavy bleeding.

The brothers tried to help him, but Kabanda signalled them not to.

'Please hear me out first. You'll soon be out of all your misery then. Continue on this path and turn southwest to reach the Pampa river. There, you will find Sabari's ashram. She's an elderly woman. She's been waiting to see you and talk to you. Please pay her a visit. All your sorrows will end, and your life will be peaceful again. The injuries you inflicted upon me aren't ordinary ones; I can feel the life ebbing out of me. I won't be able to accompany you to the ashram. Go there, but please ensure you follow the directions I have given you; they will take you to Sabari. Trust me, you'll not want to leave the banks of the Pampa once you're there. You'll feel a sense of calm wash over you once you see the beautiful forest, river, mountains and creatures. Sabari's wise words will solve all your dilemmas. Please listen to me, go there…' Kabanda lost consciousness as he spoke.

The brothers did not have the heart to leave Kabanda in the middle of the forest. They pulled his limp body towards a small hillock. They repented attempting to take Kabanda's life and waited for him to breathe his last so they could perform his final rites.

Kabanda regained consciousness one last time.

While on the one hand Kabanda's repeated pleas to visit Sabari took Rama and Lakshmana by surprise, on the other, they also raised several suspicions.

Rama looked at Kabanda in his dying moments and said, 'Kabanda! Seeing you on the brink of death because of us fills us with sorrow. But at the same time, I have a suspicion that you're trying to push us towards danger as your final act of revenge. Not that we're scared of threats. Nor do we bow before obstacles. We're well equipped and skilled enough to overcome any challenge. But we can't afford to waste any more time. My wife Sita is in deep trouble. I can't waste a single minute diverting my efforts elsewhere rather than towards looking for her. For that very reason, I'm asking you to reconsider any feelings of vengeance you may have towards us. Even though I'm giving you my word that I'll go to the banks of the Pampa, I may still go wherever my search for Sita takes me. However, it's not Arya dharma to violate a promise. I'm travelling through these wild and treacherous forests to carry out that very dharma. I request you to consider doing us good in your last minutes and attain salvation.'

After listening to Rama's predicament patiently, Kabanda said, 'Rama! I have nothing but respect for you. I'm not angry with you. After you explained your reasons for attacking me and the ordeal you've been going through with your wife's abduction, how can I possibly harbour any ill will towards you? The banks of the Pampa will soothe you. The region will help ease your trepidation and curb your impulsiveness, giving you much-needed relief. The wind and water there will help you recover from the fatigue of travel and give your heart joy.'

Rama, without a flicker of doubt, believed in Kabanda. He stole a glance at Lakshmana, whose face was still shrouded in hesitancy. Despite his excruciating pain, Kabanda noticed Lakshmana's uncertainty.

'Dear Rama and Lakshmana! In these very last minutes of mine, I shall recollect the shores of the Pampa, the splendour of the forest, the humans and other creatures inhabiting it, and its water and air. I shall try to invoke the spirit of the forest in me. I shall exit this world with serenity. The agony of my injuries vanishes the moment I think of the Pampa. It's your choice whether you go there or not. However, the mere fact that my relaying of the Pampa's vivid scenes lets you behold them in your mind's eye should ease your afflictions. You will regain your composure and return to a balanced state of mind to be able to continue looking for your wife. Listen to me…'

The brothers exchanged looks with each other before a more attentive Rama signalled to Kabanda to continue.

'Dear Rama and Lakshmana! If you go to the forests of the Pampa now, you'll behold all six seasons at once. You'll see them dancing together in harmony. Somewhere, you'll see that spring has emerged with all its companions. All around you will be trees in full bloom. The land will be carpeted with layers of flowers. The colours are so vibrant that you'll begin to wonder how many colours there truly are in the universe! I'm sure you wouldn't have seen those many hues in your life. With cuckoos singing in unison, you'll find the forest swaying to their orchestra. Even the breeze moves with utmost caution so as to not disrupt the notes of the melody.

'Elsewhere, you'd feel the sunshine and warmth of summer. You get abundant choices to feel cooler there—fruit juices and fragrant jasmine shrubs. Imagine anything that relieves you from the summer heat, and you will find it there. With all its cooling remedies, the summer season in the Pampa could at least soothe the agitation caused by your wife's absence, even if just a little. The sandalwood trees over there would embrace you.

'Aren't these the last days of the rainy season? Now, I'm sure you can imagine monsoon yourself—the beauty of dark clouds and the lightning that tears the sky apart, followed soon by the mrudangam-like beats of thunder. The cool breeze caresses your head, assuring you that there's nothing to be afraid of. The cleanest streams of rain could cleanse your physical and emotional wounds. The rainy season is indeed life-giving. Every creature and plant feels blessed after getting drenched in the rain.

'Rama! You must have seen the glories of autumn during your expeditions through the woods. Now, go and behold its beauty in the Pampa region. Your eyes won't be enough to take it all in. Neither will your heart. The splendour of the full moon on the shores is beyond human imagination. The sight is so breathtaking that even the forest seems to get goosebumps! So mesmerizing is autumn's full moon that every creature follows it. As the crystal-clear water mirrors the moon, the reflection spreads across the river, and the shadows of the trees lean in to glimpse this beauty. The Pampa cradles all of this in her cosy womb. Rama, this is a sight that enriches life.

'What can one say of the time just before winter! It is a golden period. The trees glow in a variety of amber hues. In their final stage, the leaves, satisfied with the lives they've lived, surrender to the inevitable, ready to fall. The sun's rays filter through the holes in the canopy, dissolving the lingering dew. In the sunshine, the vibrant foliage comes alive—a true spectacle. The flowers bloom in so many shades this season, it's impossible to count them all. Our ears are blessed to hear the bees, singing and sipping the nectar from these flowers. All creatures rejoice during this remarkable time, which is both warm and cool.

'Finally, the winter—most view it merely as a season when leaves fall. True, the leaves turn brown and drop to the ground. But soon, you can see the tiniest of tiny blooms emerging once again. If we take a moment to regard this verdure, all our worries and anxieties wash away; we shed who we were and transform ourselves, filling ourselves with hopes and desires. The entire mystery of this creation appears to lie within our grasp—there's a great sense of calmness, an awakening, and a release. Release from all clutches and shackles!'

Rama and Lakshmana realized that Kabanda was at the doorstep of his own release, and sadness clouded their faces.

'Looks like both of you haven't been eating well because of all your hardships. You seem exhausted and withered. Once you reach the banks of the Pampa, roast the fish, prawns and crabs available in the river, and enjoy them. The delicious taste of the fish will revive your dead tastebuds. I can tell you that you haven't eaten young deer meat that tastes like the one found in the forests of the Pampa. Even as life is ebbing out of me, my desire to live is renewed as I reminisce about its taste.

'All this aside, the divine sight and wisdom of Sabari Mata will guide you. After meeting her, please go to the Rushyamuka mountain and meet Hanuma and Sugreeva. Like you, they too are in distress. One needs friendship and a retinue when in crisis. I hope you can find ways to help each other. Who knows, seeing you and your ways of living, Sugreeva may change his mind; his obsession for rajyam may cease, and he may find peace in life. Your union will bring harmony to everyone involved. Do meet Sugreeva. He desperately needs your help.'

Kabanda paused as his breathing became laboured. He hoped Rama would be able to convince Sugreeva to banish his desires for rajyam, like Rama himself had done, abandoning the throne for his father's sake, and restore his brotherhood with Vali.

Kabanda breathed his last peacefully, satisfied that he could fulfil Sabari's wish of seeing Rama and attempt to help Sugreeva with his predicament.

As Rama and Lakshmana approached the Pampa, they felt their weariness waning.

'There seems to be something special about the air coming from the Pampa waters, Lakshmana! I already feel less tired. My body feels lighter, my steps too. If Sita had been with us, we would have camped here,' Rama said. The very name Sita made his eyes well up and his voice crack.

Placing his hand gently on his shoulder, Lakshmana comforted Rama; he urged him to stay strong.

They trekked to the top of a hillock and observed the surroundings as far as their eyes could see. There was a green island with clean waters flowing around it. The forest's profound beauty captivated the distressed brothers, offering them a glimmer of joy amid tough times.

Suddenly, something strange occurred. The tranquil waters of the Pampa began to swell, forming a pitch-black hill! Rama and Lakshmana stood frozen, dumbstruck, as they watched the water take on such a shape. Their eyes met in silent astonishment. When they gazed back at the waters again, the dark hill was swaying. The brothers could not tell if it was a hill rising from the water or the water itself had become a hill. Slowly, the moving mound edged closer, drawing near the hillock where they stood.

'Lakshmana! It's a herd of elephants, not a hill!' Rama said.

They were awestruck by the sight of tuskers of that towering height, strength and grandeur. Never before had they laid eyes on beasts of such might, and they stood spellbound as these majestic creatures played, bathed, and quenched their thirst in the river. Then, walking away with an elegant gait, the herd gradually disappeared from their view.

The brothers ventured into the waters to moisten their parched throats. The sweet water rejuvenated them. The fish sprung up to kiss their shoulders before plunging back into the river. The birds in the thick woods seemed to be orchestrating a concert for them. After having some fruits from the nearby trees, the brothers began looking for Sabari's ashram, keeping Kabanda's directions in mind. Despite their best efforts to reach sooner, dusk greeted them before they could find the ashram. Forced to continue their search only after sunrise, they had to look for a place to rest for the night.

The brothers settled under a huge tree. There were no leaves or flowers under it; it was as if someone had cleaned the spot just for them. They lit a bonfire at a distance to keep themselves warm on that chilly night.

Rama could not sleep. His mind was occupied with the unexpected events of the day. Why did he attack Kabanda? Why did he rush through his decision? Instead of forbidding him, even Lakshmana had followed suit. If only Sita had been around him to stop him from committing such follies. It was the last year of their exile, having already spent thirteen years in the forests. Only a year remained before they could return home, but then Sita was abducted. She was never keen on hurting or killing any creature. She repeatedly implored Rama to overcome his propensity to shoot an arrow at a living being without weighing the consequences and considering whether it was absolutely necessary to attack.

Rama recollected his wife's advice to him in the early days of their life in the forests.

Those were days before Rama, Sita and Lakshmana had reached Panchavati. This was when Maharshi Agastya had not spoken to Rama about the beautiful region of Panchavati and the natural forests along the banks of the Godavari. Without a fixed destination, the three wandered from one ashram to another, staying a few days in each, meeting munis and attempting to understand the troubles they were facing. In several ashrams, the munis held Rama in high regard and urged him to end the menace of Dasyarajas—rulers of smaller kingdoms in the region—who constantly disrupted their penances. Rama assured them that his Kshatriya dharma was to protect Brahmins, even without being told. So now that they had entreated him, he would undoubtedly help.

Once during their journey, they stopped at Maharshi Suteekshana's ashram. The humble abode was serene and the maharshi was at peace. After receiving his guests, the sage told his three visitors about the quiet lives of the ashram's residents. There was no mention of dangers or troubles. Although he spoke of the occasional scare of wild animals entering the ashram, the beasts were harmless and nobody was ever hurt.

Rama had an intense urge to shoot the animals that frightened the residents of the ashram with his sharp arrows, aiming to spare them from the terror. However, he knew that Suteekshana Muni was the epitome of non-violence and would not tolerate such an act. He hoped to leave the place before spotting a wild being and conveyed the same to the maharshi. The muni gave them his blessings. He told them about many places worth visiting in the forests of Dandakaranya and gave them directions to get there.

Rama noticed a perceptible difference in Sita's demeanour since arriving at this ashram and meeting Suteekshana Muni. She seemed happier but was also lost in deep thought. Rama was keen to know every thought in her mind. This was not a recent development; he had been keen on getting to know her since their wedding. Sita did not hide anything from her husband either. Even if she wanted to, she found it impossible. Her face was a reflection of everything that went on in her mind. Rama's favourite pastime was to read all that was legible on his wife's face.

When they left Suteekshana's Muni's ashram, Rama insisted on knowing what Sita was mulling over. She smiled.

'Rama, I felt that Suteekshana Muni was exceptional compared to all the sages we have met so far. I've never seen somebody so calm and composed. Others may possess greater power or lustre, but he seems unlike anyone else. So utterly serene.'

Rama agreed with Sita's observation. But he asked her why she was dwelling on something so obvious. Sita tried to be as gentle and collected as possible, and answered him with utmost care:

'The words you shared with the muni before we bid him goodbye made me ponder. Ever since we embarked on this journey through the forests, I've been reflecting on our experiences, and I'd like to share some thoughts with you. It's not that you don't already know them, but I just wanted to remind you.'

She paused and looked at Rama. The seriousness with which Sita broached the subject made him curious.

'You're someone who upholds all dharmas. You're well aware of all of them. Among those dharmas are three that a satpurush—a noble soul—should never forget. Again, you know them all, and yet I'd like to remind you of one of those only to help you stay vigilant.'

'What is it?' Rama's response was dry. He was unable to follow Sita's train of thought. To not be able to understand her was insufferable to Rama.

'One thing is certain: you adhere to the truth with an unwavering commitment, embracing it in its purest and most stringent form. No one comes close to you in this regard. You wouldn't violate the truth even in your dreams, let alone for the sake of jest. The second one is desiring others' wives. I know that such a thought would never cross your mind. The third and final one is non-violence. No one can be entirely non-violent. I understand that one may resort to violence out of necessity—to secure food or to protect oneself or others from danger. But it's forbidden, even in thought, to harm another without reason.

'You said that you'd guard the munis of Dandakaranya by slaying the rakshasas. It wasn't a mere assurance; you pledged it. Only a short while ago, you told Suteekshana Muni that you wouldn't spare a wild animal, and only because he discourages violence, you hastily took his leave. We left his ashram sooner than planned. I'm anxious for you. I'm sure you know those who carry weapons are often eager to use them. When we possess extraordinary power, we're inclined to use it. It's a natural human impulse.

'But the mark of truly great men lies in their ability to curb this impulse, to wield their power wisely and only when the situation truly demands it. I long to see you as such a great man. I'm repeating myself. It's not that you're not aware of these truths. But I thought it best to remind you.'

Sita had divulged to her husband everything that was on her mind. Rama thought for a while and said, 'Sita! I appreciate all that you shared with me. But I can't promise I'd abide by your principles.'

Sita looked at Rama in surprise. This was the first time he had denied her wish.

'The first and foremost dharma is to protect the truth. I promised the maharshis that I'd protect the Brahmins by killing the rakshasas, which means I will have to do so. If I don't, won't my promise to them be broken?'

'Yes, I'm worried about the pledge. Going to Dandakaranya doesn't feel right. It's unwise to attack the people over there when you bear no enmity against them. I can't accept killing those who never harmed us.'

'Sita! I'm a Kshatriya. I belong to a royal clan. It is my dharma to safeguard those in distress. I'm obliged to follow this dharma regardless of where I am.'

'Rama, we live in the forest. Let us live like the sages, devoting ourselves to penance and rituals. You may resume your duties as a Kshatriya once we're back in Ayodhya.'

'No, Sita! I promised the Brahmins that I'd save them from the Dasyas. I can't go back on my word. It's not even a mere promise, it was my pledge to them. Sita, I can forgo my life, or my other life Lakshmana, or even you—you, who is dearer to me than my own life. But I can't go back on the pledge, particularly the one made to Brahmins.'

Realizing that the situation had gone beyond her control, Sita remained silent, crestfallen.

Rama's heart was filled with turmoil. Turning Sita down was distressing for him.

'Sita, I know you shared all your concerns with me for my own good. And I have, in turn, shared with you my perception of responsibility. Let's try to understand each other's point of view and end this conversation here.'

He gently touched Sita's shoulder. Sita continued to be silent. She never brought the topic up again.

Rama recollected this exchange with Sita while resting in the forests of the Pampa. Sita's caution that one would use weapons mindlessly just because they possessed them turned out to be true in Kabanda's case. He had killed a good man. Sita would be distraught if she found out about it.

Rama's heart grew heavier with Sita's memories.

Rama's mission, of either eliminating the Dasyarajas from the forest or taking them into the fold of Arya dharma, was in progress. Meanwhile, Sita had been kidnapped. He sought rivalry with Ravana and perhaps even a war! But he had anticipated that Ravana would attack him with his troops, never that he would abduct Sita! Ravana knew that Sita was dearer to Rama than his own life. Killing Ravana was inevitable now, but it wouldn't be that easy. Lakshmana and he alone would not be able to find out where Ravana was holding Sita captive. It would be excellent if Sugreeva, whom Kabanda had spoken about, could help them. But why had Kabanda asked him to meet Sabari first instead of Sugreeva? Was this some kind of evil scheme to get them into further trouble?

Always at his brother's service, Lakshmana was more vigilant during the nights. Seeing that Rama was still awake, he gently reminded him to rest. Nobody else understood his brother's turmoil like Lakshmana did. The screeches of the wild animals echoed through the forest. The certainty that the sun would rise soon brought Rama some comfort, allowing him to sleep, if only for a little while.

With the first rays of the sun, Sabari bathed in the waters of the Pampa, observed the mesmerizing sunrise, bowed in reverence to the omniscient witness and returned to her ashram. Of late, her stamina had dropped significantly.

Even the simple act of taking a bath had become a great ordeal, draining her energy. Yet, her eyes were brimming with the hope that Rama and Lakshmana would arrive any moment.

Bone-tired, Sabari was resting in her abode when she heard someone asking, 'Is this Sabari Mata's ashram?'

She was startled by the question and eagerly stepped out of her dwelling. Before her were two young men, their tall frames and broad shoulders commanding attention.

'Sons, are you Rama and Lakshmana?' she asked in a quivering voice.

'Yes, Mata. Kabanda directed us to meet you here.'

Sabari, with her eyes wide open, watched them from head to toe. She continued to hold on to her hope of having them as her advocates.

'Come, sons, come,' she welcomed them. After they had seated themselves, Sabari placed before them a bowl of fruits.

'I know the sweetest fruits in this forest. For many years now, we've been surviving on them. I kept the best fruits from our pickings aside for your sake. You won't get such delicious fruits anywhere else. Have them, sons. We have many things to discuss after your hunger is satiated.'

Both brothers ate to their hearts' content and drank fresh water. Then, Rama asked what Sabari had been meaning to talk to them about.

'Kabanda told us you've been waiting for us. How do you know about us? What do you know? What made you anticipate our arrival?'

'Rama, Sutapa, from the city of Ayodhya, told me about you sacrificing your throne. In times when kings are endangering the earth out of greed for power and kingship, you both have abandoned your rajyam to live in the forests. I was looking forward to seeing you. My hope is that you will guide mankind into times when there would be no kingdoms, no cities, no civilization. Matanga Maharshi has departed already, and my time will be up soon. You're young and capable. During your expeditions through the forests, you should inform people about the perils of nagarikata and motivate them to live in harmony with nature instead. I've been waiting for you, hoping to convince you of this purpose,' Sabari said.

Rama and Lakshmana looked at each other in surprise. Sabari narrated to them incidents from her childhood, the forced occupations, her parents' death, and the physical and mental torture inflicted on Matanga.

'We'd like to live as we did in my childhood. In those days, we were unaware of wars. We experienced every possible human feeling and emotion in their purest forms, from hunger and tasting good food to bearing the pain of physical injuries. We wandered the woods freely without restrictions; border forces was a concept unknown to us. There were no boundary walls or fences. We've lost that world—no, actually, we didn't; the nagariks seized it from us. The civilized drove us out of our own homes. When we attempted to make our way in again, they punished us for not being their subjects or belonging to the cities. They captured us and put us through great torture. Why does the earth need borders? Who made these senseless rules that labelled us as the "ruled" in a place where we were born? Who are they to impose such hierarchies? What's their power over us?...' Exhausted and panting, Sabari took a few moments to contain her emotions.

Rama looked at Sabari as if he had arrived at a conclusion.

'Mata! You're trying to spin the wheel of time backwards, and that's impossible. Besides, you have some gross misunderstanding about me. I'm from Ayodhya, a nagaravasi, and I've been abiding by the dharma of nagarikata from the moment I was born. I didn't abandon my rajyam forever. My life in the forest is motivated by a strong desire to expand the territories of the Aryas. In the thirteen years I've been in the forest, I've strived hard to train the aranyavasis in the civilized ways of the Aryas.

'Recently, a Dasyaraja abducted my wife. I came here searching for her. I'll kill the man who kidnapped my wife in the war, occupy his rajyam, and only then return to Ayodhya. I'd continue to rule over my own rajyam. You think nagarikata is destruction, while I want to be remembered as the maryada purushottam, the best among honourable men, who won't stand for anything but that.

'Sita's abduction came as an unexpected obstacle, but it is only making me more determined and driving me towards executing my duties better. I can't be a part of your hopes and aspirations.'

Rama's calm and composed words pierced Sabari like sharp arrows.

'Rama! It's indeed tragic that your wife has been kidnapped. Perhaps the Dasyaraja holds some grudge against you to have abducted her in such a manner. Rajyams, after all, breed enmity.

'Have I not just shared with you my own story, Rama? My mother, my father, and I—barely ten years old—were on our way to visit my grandfather in the forest. We were captured by nagariks and turned into slaves. I was a child, with no one to look for me. No one to seek revenge for all the ways I'd been wronged. And I don't think you can truly grasp the pain I endured. But I can—I can imagine the depth of your sorrow over Sita's abduction, Rama. I sincerely hope you're reunited with her soon. At the same time, I hope you find a way to free yourself from the chains of nagarikata as well...'

The wrinkles on Sabari's face deepened. The tears in her eyes softened Rama.

'Mata, please think about human life and understand that the ultimate purpose is to make humans civilized, turn them into nagariks. In the process, it is possible that a few may be uprooted from their current situations. If you can welcome that change, you won't be in pain. But if you try to resist the change, it will hurt you,' he said.

Sabari looked at Rama with pity. Her voice was laced with a subtle tremor, as she put her thoughts forward:

'Change is always occurring. In a slow, silent and beautiful way, change has been occurring and it will continue to do so. But you're all meddling with its process. And because of the interference of you nagariks, not just humans but every other being on the planet—the waterbodies, the trees, the mountains alike—are suffering too. Everything and everyone is being subjected to violence. I'm simply asking you to try and stop that intrusion. Thus far, nature has prospered only through collaboration. Instead, the civilized ways are driven by force and hostility, and everything that is integral to nature is being looted. You are encouraging these measures. Who told you that we can't change for the better if we cooperate with one another? We don't need this mad rush. What we need is tranquillity and steadiness. Our existence would be blessed only if we followed the laws of nature.'

Rama and Lakshmana shifted slightly, displaying their impatience. They could find no meaning in Sabari's arguments.

'All of you are so engrossed in making inventions and newer weapons that you're forgetting to create goodness.'

'What is "goodness" anyway, Mata?' asked Rama. 'Can you provide an unambiguous definition of good? The definition keeps changing with time and because of time.'

A smile bloomed on Sabari's face. The whole essence of goodness shone on her face.

'Why do you say that, son? Good means being careful and responsible towards the creation we all live in, right? You all have forgotten the basics. You act as if all of nature is on one side and you're on the other. Rama, aren't we, too, a part of this infinite universe? As humans, we can think, talk and find new ways of living. But for that very reason, because we possess such precious powers, we should be more responsible towards nature. Shouldn't we remind ourselves of our strengths and use them for the greater good—isn't that the goodness we should aspire for? If you abandon that responsibility and the freedom needed to carry it out, and instead create rules, restrictions, territories, borders, identities, authorities and governing principles, aren't you confining yourselves? The whole of nature is being destroyed. You must do away with the thought that as humans you're different from the rest of nature. Come, become one with nature.'

Rama was taken aback by the spark on Sabari's face, but her words still did not make any sense to him.

'Mata, I shall think about what you said. I'll discuss your arguments with my gurus. Rajyams are formed to look after their people, to treat them well. I've taken an oath to that effect. I feel a great sense of responsibility towards anyone under my rule. For now, I have a duty towards my wife, to rescue her from captivity. I have to return to my rajyam and guard it with a thousand eyes.'

Rama stood up. Taking the hint, Lakshmana followed suit. Sabari, however, did not move the slightest.

'Rama! You're full of jnanam, and I'm ripe with ajnanam. I have only one more thing to tell you. The rajyam can't protect anyone; it doesn't grant anyone freedom. You're able to fulfil your duty towards your wife only because you're unburdened by the rule of any rajyam right now. But once you reclaim your throne, your freedom would be tethered, and the very wish to protect your wife or even to be by her side will slip beyond your reach. How can you protect your subjects when you can't guarantee the same for your kin? The rajyam only fosters irresponsibility and stringent behaviour. The thirst for power and control takes a toll on all who seek them!'

Having nothing to offer in response to Sabari, Rama and Lakshmana bowed to her and walked out of the ashram.

As the ray of hope that Sabari had held on to so desperately was doused, she gently slumped to one side.

Sabari had fulfilled her duty on earth with care, love and freedom till her very last breath.

IN CONVERSATION

Volga and Purnima Tammireddy

P.S.

Insights,
Interviews &
More. . .

Purnima Tammireddy: Your previous works, *The Liberation of Sita* and *Yashodhara*, are also retellings of myth-history, like the present book. As a reader, I also see a progression of themes in these three works. While *The Liberation of Sita* is about how patriarchy treats women and emphasizes the need for sisterhood to counter it, *Yashodhara* delves into the philosophical and spiritual meaning of human existence. *On the Banks of the Pampa* takes the discourse a step further, urging us to be more responsible towards nature and reminding us humbly how inconsequential our existence is in the grand scheme of things.

Do you see these three works as a trilogy? Were they planned to be one?

Volga: I didn't plan these three works as a trilogy. *The Liberation of Sita* emphasizes sisterhood, but the central theme I wished to convey through it was the concept of power—how it operates in every relationship. Power is all-pervasive, and in these stories, I sought to explore the power of the state, the throne, Brahminism, and the power that operates within human emotions and relationships.

My primary focus is to help readers understand that we should neither submit to power wielded by others nor wield power over others. In recognizing this, women will come to see the value of sisterhood.

In *Yashodhara*, I aimed to transform the image of Yashodhara from one of victimhood to that of an agent of change. She stands not as a passive figure but as a comrade of Siddhartha—an early woman-philosopher and spiritual seeker. While it is true that women have been victims of patriarchy, they are also fighting back—through their intellect, sense of humour, anger, patience, love, and yes, even their innocence. These are the very qualities they have used to bring about change. I wanted to portray Yashodhara as a force of transformation, for it was her determination that, for the first time, allowed women to enter the spiritual realm as bhikkhunis.

Pampateeram addresses the relationship between humans and nature. It examines how hegemonic power, especially one that's wielded by men, is used to destroy nature in the name of development. Men have treated nature as a slave, an entity to conquer and control, rather than as a friend and saviour.

In this process of destruction, the state plays a significant role. It exists to protect the hegemonic structures humans have created in the name of civilization—structures built on greed, authority, race, religion, caste, borders and nations. These constructs are ultimately costing both nature and humanity, which are inextricably linked.

I do not, however, believe humans are inconsequential in the grand scheme of things. In the course of our evolution, we've emerged as beings with the capacity to save or destroy other life forms and the environment. We have intelligence, creativity and innovation in our possession. Because of these qualities, we must be more concerned, compassionate and humane towards nature and the earth.

Purnima Tammireddy: What are some of the challenges you face as a writer while taking a known story into unknown directions?

Volga: '... taking a known story into unknown directions'—do we know the whole story? Do we know the text we read? Does the story in the text really end, or does it offer numerous insights and open up new directions to begin afresh?

After reading, listening to and viewing the Ramayana in its various forms, I see many apertures or windows through which I can look into it. The 'drushyam' I perceive and encounter when I read a myth is entirely different from its conventional understandings and interpretations. Suddenly, my thoughts focus on something new and search for unknown paths to realize or reach that drushyam. I don't have to worry about losing my way, because it's a familiar direction to me, one I have been on many times—a feminist direction. I travelled in that direction and it unravelled things hidden in the hearts of women in mythology, particularly in the Ramayana. Valmiki, the great writer, gave us many open endings and little puzzles, and when one attempts to connect the dots and solve those puzzles, new stories are born.

The feminist lens gives me different viewpoints not in the original text. But I respect the original text; that is the main source of light for my journey in this direction. The respect and love I have for the text and its characters makes my journey easy. The inner thoughts of these women characters come to light and show me the beauty of hitherto unknown paths and directions.

So, I never felt challenged when I wrote these stories taken from the Ramayana. They just flowed from my heart through my pen. I was truly content and tranquil while travelling in these directions.

Purnima Tammireddy: Where and how did the seed for this story emerge? Why did you choose Sabari to be the protagonist here?

Volga: Sabari—that name itself is beautiful to me. In the Valmiki Ramayana, there are only four shlokas about Sabari. But across the varied narrative forms of the Ramayana in Telugu, in films and literature, Sabari's character is highlighted. She is included in considerable detail in a number of movie songs. She is the incarnation of bhakti. Modern Telugu poets like Devulapalli, Krishna Shastri and Arudra depict beautifully the way she awaits Rama's arrival with a profound longing and hope in her heart. These songs and poems are immensely popular … All the emotions woven around her character made her unforgettable.

I always wondered why Sabari waited for Rama. How did she know about Rama? Rama was not known in the far south at the time. There was little chance of the great tales of his valour and spirit reaching that far. He had only been married and then exiled to the forest. Even Hanuma and Sugreeva hadn't known about him. How did Sabari know? What was the reason behind her becoming such an ardent devotee of Rama? … All these questions bothered me.

For sure, Sabari was a tribal woman. She was a disciple of Matanga Maharshi, who was from an untouchable community. How did they meet? Why did Sabari turn into his shishya? What were the issues that bothered them at a time when the state was growing more powerful even in forest areas? When Aryans were invading and spreading their culture, why did Sabari wait for Rama, an Aryan king? What did she want to tell him?

With these questions about Sabari and with many other contemporary questions about the environment, deforestation, civilization, state, citizenship, borders and boundaries, and my feminist political perspective, I started my journey into the forest where Sabari lived. Slowly and steadily, I found my way and finally landed at Sabari's ashram, where the whole story unfolded.

Purnima Tammireddy: It seems you're championing the need for dialogue and conversations in all your works. In *The Liberation of Sita*, Sita gets to talk with Ahalya and Surpanakha, characters she otherwise doesn't meet. In *Yashodhara*, Siddhartha constantly engages with his wife on philosophical topics. In this book, however, Rama/Sugreeva and Sabari have a huge chasm between them, but you still find a middle ground for them to have a dialogue.

Do you think we can solve/resolve many of the issues that plague our society through consistent and sincere dialogue?

Volga: I used conversations mostly in *The Liberation of Sita*, not in *On the Banks of the Pampa*. But I believe conversations are important to know each other and to learn from each other. This is also a kind of style I use in some stories, particularly when every character has something important to say and share. I'm not inclined to make these important points as part of narration.

Yes, dialogue is the need of the hour. Nowadays everyone prefers monologues. I'm keen on breaking these silos. Our ideas and views need to be challenged, and we must be provoked to have a healthy discussion, which will eventually lead to a discourse among larger sections of the people.

Usually, we tend to share with those whose views are similar to ours. It may give us strength. But we also have to listen to those who have a different point of view, think and discuss those views. Only then will our horizons be widened.

Purnima Tammireddy: Agreed. Either online or offline, more and more of us are unwittingly becoming part of echo chambers—where we hear only what we like to hear. Any challenge posed to a person's ideas and views is often misconstrued as an attack on their identity or community. In such chaotic times, keeping our views to ourselves and remaining silent seems a safer and saner option! To loan a phrase from Italo Calvino, 'dialogues between the deaf'—what's the point? But this novel made me hopeful about speaking up even when there's no hope.

However, neither Rama nor Sugreeva even makes an attempt to understand Sabari's philosophy. Though she earnestly tries to engage in a conversation with them, they just prefer to walk away. What happens to Sabari's voice then? How do you view Sabari's dissent? Why do you think it's important to raise a voice even when it's likely to go unheard?

Volga: The voice of dissent, once recorded, will be heard—somewhere, sometime. To speak, to raise one's voice, to put forth thoughts is the bare minimum, the foundational act of our responsibility. For we possess the ability to think, to speak, and to record through countless forms. Throughout history, there have been many Sabaris beyond the Sabari of the Ramayana. From Sabari to the Chipko movement, to Janu, Vandana Shiva, Sunita Narain, to the tribal women battling for their survival and the survival of nature—the continuity is undeniable. We must recognize this continuity and do our duty.

These voices of dissent are not mere echoes, they are the lifeblood of human history.

Purnima Tammireddy: Kabanda, in the Ramayana, is a deformed rakshasa, but you present him here as devoid of any physical shortcomings, and only in a sentence or two. About Sabari, too, there's not much physical description. Can you elaborate on how you approach descriptions of your characters?

Volga: There wasn't much of a scope to describe Kabanda's body in this novel. If the story had needed it, I might have provided greater detail. Similarly, for the description of the main character, Sabari, I hardly used five or six sentences in the entire text.

Usually in my stories, physical characteristics occupy very little space. If the descriptions help in taking the story forward, or if the story needs those details, only then I will include them. I use most of the space in the text to put forward my new ideas and insights. Especially in short stories and short novels, using the space economically and judiciously is very important. I use my space with much care. My stories are so tightly structured that no word can be removed. If you do, you lose something I want to emphasize.

In this short novel, I used a lot of space to describe the forest, which is the most important character in the story. Without the description of the forest, there is no story.

Purnima Tammireddy: During the editing phases of this translation, we also discussed the importance of brevity in the retellings of the myths. Except for briefly mentioning a few critical developments, you don't delve deep into them. For example, the backstory of why the brothers, Vali and Sugreeva, are vying for each other's blood. Or, why and how Ravana abducted Sita. Could you please elaborate on your process of sticking to the main story of Sabari and Matanga Muni, and leaving out other relevant but not so compulsory parts in this narrative?

Volga: The stories about Vali, Sugreeva, the abduction of Sita are known to Indian readers, the common people and non-literate people. For the youngest generation who may not know the Ramayana, there are many books and various media through which they can learn the story.

My focus was to tell the story I wanted to tell—Sabari's and Matanga Muni's. Their names may be familiar but their stories were not written with the depth they deserve. They were outcastes and tribals who stood for protecting nature and their own self-respect. Sabari and Matanga are not remembered as voices of dissent against empires, states and the so-called civilization. And so, I held on to that story.

Purnima Tammireddy: Your Telugu prose is quite exquisite. The descriptions of scenic beauty (especially in

On the Banks of the Pampa) read like prose-poetry. As a novelist, how do you craft your prose? One that is accessible to contemporary readers while also justifying a mythical/ancient setting?

Volga: I'm a literature student. I read epics and kavyas in Telugu. I've read all great writers in Telugu. Those great treasures of literature taught me how to use language with felicity.

Using appropriate words is the first step you have to learn when you start writing. I think I'm learning it with each of my books. It gives me great happiness to see the difference in the language I used in *The Liberation of Sita*, *Yashodhara* and *On the Banks of the Pampa*. Each is written according to its theme and characters. Telugu is a beautiful language. It is classically rich, full of beautiful dialects, and is musical in how it sounds. I think I love my Telugu and Telugu loves me.

Purnima Tammireddy: Indeed, Telugu loves you!

Your love for good stories is also no secret. The fact that you've been a prolific translator throughout your career, bringing some stellar national and international literature to Telugu doesn't get as much attention as your other contributions. I wish it would!

The translations of your works have reached far and wide, and gained you readers across the country. They have gone on to win prestigious awards like the Kendra Sahitya Akademi award … How do you perceive translations in general—their importance? What do they mean to you?

Volga: Translations hold a special place in my heart. I grew up reading translated works from across the world. I devoured them so completely that they became a part of me. Without reading the Ramayana and Mahabharata in simple and accessible Telugu, without exploring the works of Mark Twain, Tolstoy, Maxim Gorky, Jack London, Sharatchandra, Tagore, Premchand, Sivasankara Pillai, Pannalal Patel, Bibhutibhushan Bandyopadhyay, to name just a few—I wouldn't have been who I am today. Their writings are the nourishment for my soul, alongside Telugu literature.

Purnima Tammireddy: Unlike between the Indian languages, there's no shared culture and idiom between Telugu and English. Especially, in a text like *On the Banks of the Pampa*, the story relies heavily on terms/concepts like 'nagarikata', 'jnanam', 'ajnanam', etc. Initially, in the first draft, I'd tried to translate these words into English. I'd used 'civilization', 'wisdom', 'ignorance'. Upon reviewing the text, we decided to retain some Telugu words in the translated text too. In Matanga Muni's story, we've retained 'jati' as it is and refrained from translating it as 'caste' ... In such a case, what according to you are the opportunities and/or limitations when your works are being translated into English? What do you hope they will capture? What do you think they won't?

Volga: It depends. In the act of translation, we're crossing many a barrier—of language, of culture, of socio-political history—all at once. And because of these unyielding constraints, sometimes we may get only fifty per cent of what the writer intended to tell in the translation. But that's okay. I'd say, take that fifty per cent—it's better than having nothing. As readers, if we put enough mind and heart into the text we're reading, we'd still understand everything that the writer had to share from the something we got in the translation. Nothing is no good. Don't you agree?

And yes, I believe retaining some of the Telugu words as they were was critical to this novel. It's not that there are no equivalent words for these in English—there are, as your first draft showed—but they don't carry the same weight and history as they do in Telugu.

For example, 'jati' in Telugu was (and is still being) used with a meaning that emphasizes the upper strata in caste and religion. Sometimes, it also means race. One of the phrases used in Telugu to refer to Dalits is 'kada jati'. 'Kada' means last in the hierarchical order and thereby the implication that Dalits are distant from the upper strata. Expressions such as, 'Neeku neeti, jati leda?'—Don't you have neeti (morals/ethics) and jati?—show how languages become carriers of deep-rooted discrimination and othering. So, when you first translated 'jati' as 'tribe', I felt it was better to retain the Telugu word as it is. Likewise, for the other important words in the text.

I'm happy with the translations of my works. I'm grateful that my stories reach new readers of different languages because of these translations.

On the Banks of the Pampa may seem like a slim book, but it's quite a challenge to translate. I really appreciate the time, effort and patience you've put into it.

Now, why did you pick this book? What was your experience like while translating this book?

Purnima Tammireddy: Thank you for your kind words. I was never fooled by the book's size; even before the opportunity to translate it arose, I sensed the depth of the ideas you were presenting and the intricate tapestry of the story you had woven. My initial hesitation in picking up this work stemmed solely from doubt—doubt that I could do it justice.

Translating a story set in an ancient, mythological era is always a challenge. One has to move away from the contemporary influences of the language while still building a world that feels vivid and accessible to the readers. This novel, however, posed a few additional challenges. Through a series of juxtapositions, Sabari invites us to reconsider reductive binaries: jnanam–ajnanam, nagarikata–anagarikata, dharma–adharma, and the like. As we discussed, retaining certain Telugu words and phrases in the translation was essential to preserving the text's integrity.

As a simple example, when during her conversation with Rama Sabari says, '… border forces was a concept unknown to us', one might be tempted to use 'alien to us' and 'foreign to us' instead, but such choices would misalign Sabari's worldview. I had to remain vigilant to ensure that no word or phrase, however seemingly minor, betrayed the core of the aranyavasis' philosophy.

The greatest challenge of all, however, was translating passages that were breathtakingly poetic, particularly your descriptions of the Pampa forests. I can only hope—and pray—that the readers grasp at least the visual imagery in the translation, if not the enchantment of your prose.

Your support throughout this project has been invaluable. While I've translated a few works so far, my other authors—Manto, Amrita Pritam, Mallu Swarajyam—belong to a different time and era and I had to engage with their work solely through their text. At Elami Publications, I had the privilege of working with you on two books you translated, both as publisher and editor, and learned a great deal about the art of translation from you. With *On the Banks of the Pampa*, I had the opportunity to gain a closer, deeper understanding of you as a fiction writer. The project enhanced my understanding of world-building, the art of retelling myths, characterization and, most importantly, the delicate balance of knowing what to say—and what to leave unsaid.

Volga: Since you actively translate both into Telugu and from it, I'm interested to learn about it. Have you noticed any differences in translating from English to Telugu and vice versa?

Purnima Tammireddy: The usual discourse around this topic suggests that translating between Indian languages is a lot easier than into English. However, my experience has been different.

We tend to search for equivalent elements in the target language and judge its inadequacies based on what's missing. That is why, as compared to Indian languages, we think English—a colonial import and the language of the urban elite even today—is more limiting in carrying our stories. But having worked in both directions, I can confidently say that no translation is a cakewalk. Every source and target language pair throws a set of unique challenges. For instance, translating between Hindustani and Telugu can be particularly tricky. Concepts like passive voice and possessive forms are tough to render accurately. While Telugu does have these grammatical structures, they are often considered as archaic and no longer used in contemporary prose.

One thing that struck me while translating fiction into English—both this work and a few of my short stories—is how profoundly language shapes our thinking and, consequently, our storytelling. What can be left unsaid, implied between the lines, and what needs to be stated explicitly depend heavily on the language we're writing into.

Volga: That's one thing we have in common—juggling between writing fiction and taking up translations. Are there times when you feel like you're sacrificing your creative time to translate others? Why do you think some writers can't resist doing translations?

Purnima Tammireddy: I'm constantly reminded that I should do less translation and focus more on my 'own' writing. I was even advised not to publish my translation of Manto as my first book, because, apparently, once I'm recognized as a translator, my other works won't be taken seriously. It's better to build one's reputation as a ‘writer who also translates’ than a ‘translator who writes’, I was told.

Isn’t it funny how we, within the literary community, also fall for these reductionist tropes: original-translation, author-translator, created-derived, primary-secondary and so on? The creative world thrives on hierarchies, its pretensions notwithstanding.

When I write fiction, yes, I possess the ethical, moral and legal rights to it in a worldly sense. I can defend my copyright or someone can cancel me for a story I’ve written. But is it truly *my* story? Do I really own it?

To quiet all this noise, I tell myself a story: All stories are birds, and all storytellers are the trees on which these winged creatures are temporary guests. In the brief time they stay with us, if they share a story or two of theirs, and if we manage to pass those stories along to the world, that’s all there is to this creative exercise.

Some of us who can’t resist translating must be the trees that don’t discriminate between the stories—*ours* and *theirs*. Through my fiction and that of others, I feel blessed to host these stories within me. For me, all writing is translation, and all translation is writing.

I’m glad I could shelter *On the Banks of the Pampa* in me, because I see it as the ultimate expansion and extension of the feminist ideology as it highlights the violence humans inflict on nature. In this context, I have another question for you. As someone who has been writing with the lens of feminism throughout her career, how do you see climate change and environmental imbalances created by capitalist developments? Please share your comments on the fact that as humans we forget that we're part of nature and not a force against it.

Volga: Yes, I totally agree. The destruction happening around us is on a gigantic scale. All the natural resources are being destroyed for the profits of corporate companies. In the name of development, most people's lives are being disturbed and their livelihoods taken away from them. The imbalance we created in nature is making life harder. Traditionally, women have been seen and considered as nature. Therefore, violence against nature reflects violence against women. Not that men are exempted. But women are the most vulnerable and affected. The state that should protect natural resources is enabling the corporates in their exploits. So I want to examine and explore the disposition of the state and the stand it takes when it comes to protecting nature and people against capitalist interests.

I wanted to explore how under the pretext of civilization, nature is being destroyed. Only certain sections of people called their knowledge as the 'only and ultimate' knowledge system. The knowledge we can gather by interacting directly with nature and the kind of experience we can gain through such interactions are invaluable, but no one cares about all that. The fundamental questions that need to be raised but have been neglected for long are: What is knowledge? What is civilization?

Instead of asking the right questions and seeking answers to them, all of us are in a mad race towards so-called development. And so-called knowledge and so-called civilization are promoted as the ultimate goals to achieve this development. I want to question this understanding of ours.

Of course, I'm exploring these questions from a feminist perspective. I may not have the answers today but future generations must constantly seek them. Unless they come up with some answers, a lot of violence against nature will continue to happen, eventually leading to the destruction of the human race.

Purnima Tammireddy: In your note in the Telugu edition, you said you were reluctant to publish this book for a while. Why was that so?

Volga: Yes, I was when it was finally finished.

Do people understand? Are they ready to think? Will they engage in a discussion? Because everyone is enthusiastic and running with ideas of corporate development and technological advancement. Nobody is questioning the greed that is developing like water hyacinths in the human psyche. Not a lot of people are asking, 'Development for whom? Technology for what?' Time, space, speed, energy—do people comprehend how to value them? Do they try to lead their lives with a complete understanding and respect towards the laws of nature? Are they using these natural forces for the welfare of human life on this planet?

Overwhelmed by these thoughts, I felt there is not much hope. But as a writer, it's my responsibility to tell the stories I must tell. I have to make my statement. So, finally I published it. My readers received it well. They appreciated the novel, and the questions it is trying to raise.

Purnima Tammireddy: Looking at most of the fiction you've written up to this point, it seems like you're most inclined towards female protagonists to tell your stories. Would you ever consider a male protagonist?

Also, what's your next book?

Volga: It is because of my feminist perspective and politics that I choose female protagonists in my writings. Maybe I know women better than men. What troubles me is the recurrence of women characters as victims, sacrificing themselves constantly, in literature. Such characterization is caricaturish. I strive to break that trope through my female characters. But who knows. I may choose male protagonists in my future work. Why not?

As for my next book, I'm planning to start a novel, but it's too soon to divulge any details.

TRANSLATOR'S ACKNOWLEDGEMENTS

Like it takes a village to raise a child, it takes a village to bring a translation to life. I am deeply grateful to everyone who made the journey of translating *Pampateeram* not only possible but also an enriching experience.

First and foremost, the trust placed in me by Volga, the author, turned this project into more than just a translation—it became a collaboration filled with insights, learning and shared moments.

The belief in this work and the encouragement to embrace the challenge came from Rahul Soni and Arshia Sattar, whose faith in my abilities motivated me to fully commit to this project.

Rinita Banerjee's sharp insights and meticulous edits breathed clarity and precision into the text, ensuring the delicate balance between staying true to the original work and making it accessible to readers. She also became a translator-buddy, sharing both her expertise and camaraderie. Ananya M's thoughtful feedback on the first draft too proved invaluable, offering fresh perspectives that helped me refine the manuscript.

Friends like Gireesh K, Srinivas V, Subhashri DV, Radhika M, Shyamala H and others, who share a passion for translation, stood by me through thick and thin. Their support, both quiet and vocal, has been invaluable.

Ramesh Karthik Nayak has been a constant presence in my life—a reliable anchor through every tide. His support was pivotal in helping this project meet its deadlines.

My sister Sushmitha's dedication in managing Elami Publications allowed me the space to immerse myself in the translation. Her quiet, steadfast support behind the scenes made all the difference.

The beautiful cover design by Veer Misra captured the spirit of the book with elegance and depth, adding a visual narrative that complements the words within.

Finally, this work is dedicated to Sai Padma, who was a dear friend and mentor. Though you left us too soon, your belief in me continues to inspire every word I write.

My deepest gratitude to all.

—Purnima Tammireddy

ABOUT THE AUTHOR

VOLGA is a writer, critic, translator and poet, who has been a forerunner in introducing a feminist perspective into the literary-political discourse of the Telugu-speaking states. One of the most significant figures in Telugu literature today, her works opened the floodgates for a host of women writers to articulate the doubts and confusions they experienced as women. Her novel *Svecchha* (Freedom) marks a watershed in women's writing in Telugu and is now being published in all Indian languages by the National Book Trust of India. Her other works include the short-story collection *Rajakiya Kathalu* (Political Stories), which looks at the oppression of and control on a woman's body; *Maaku Godalu Levu* (We Have No Walls), the first volume in feminist philosophy in Telugu, which she edited; and an anthology of feminist poems, *Neeli Meghalu* (Dark Clouds), also one she edited. She co-authored *Saramsam*, which documents the anti-arrack struggle, and *Mahilavaranam* (Womanscape), a detailed collective biography of important Telugu women of the twentieth century. With works like *Atadu Ame Manam* (He–She–Us) and *Sahita* (Inclusion), she has contributed richly to feminist literary criticism. Volga has translated several important texts into Telugu, such as Agnes Smedley's autobiographical novel, *Daughter of Earth*, as *Bhumi Putrika*. She has also written screenplays for Telugu films, composed lyrics for dance ballets like *War and Peace*, and represented India in women's conferences in China and the United States.

She has received numerous awards and honours, including the Sahitya Akademi Award for her short-story volume, *Vimukta* (published in translation as *The Liberation of Sita*), the South Asia Ladli Media and Advertising Award for Gender Sensitivity 2015–2016, and an honorary doctorate from Sri Padmavati Women's University.

Volga lives in Hyderabad.

ABOUT THE TRANSLATOR

PURNIMA TAMMIREDDY is a writer, translator and publisher, working in both Telugu and English. She was a writer-in-residence at the 2022 Sangam House International Writer Residency. She has translated into Telugu Manto's *Siya Hashiye* and Amrita Pritam's *Pinjar*. Her English translation of the memoir of Mallu Swarajyam, the leader of the Telangana Peasants' Armed Struggle, is forthcoming. She is also the author of the short-story collection, *Emotional Pregnancy*.

In 2022, Purnima founded Elami Publications, an independent Telugu publishing house, and co-founded pustakam.net, a website for book reviews, in 2009. A techie by profession, she currently lives in Bengaluru.

ALSO BY VOLGA

The Liberation of Sita,
trans. T. Vijay Kumar & C. Vijayasree

Yashodhara: A Novel,
trans. P.S.V. Prasad

Telugu: The Best Stories of Our Times (as editor),
trans. Alladi Uma & M. Sridhar

HarperCollins *Publishers* India

At HarperCollins India, we believe in telling the best stories and finding the widest readership for our books in every format possible. We started publishing in 1992; a great deal has changed since then, but what has remained constant is the passion with which our authors write their books, the love with which readers receive them, and the sheer joy and excitement that we as publishers feel in being a part of the publishing process.

Over the years, we've had the pleasure of publishing some of the finest writing from the subcontinent and around the world, including several award-winning titles and some of the biggest bestsellers in India's publishing history. But nothing has meant more to us than the fact that millions of people have read the books we published, and that somewhere, a book of ours might have made a difference.

As we look to the future, we go back to that one word—a word which has been a driving force for us all these years.

Read.

Harper Collins · 4th · HARPER FICTION · HARPER NON-FICTION · HARPER BUSINESS · HCCB HARPERCOLLINS CHILDREN'S BOOKS

HARPER DESIGN · Harper Sport · HARPER PERENNIAL · HARPER VANTAGE · हार्पर हिन्दी · BOOKTOPUS